"Don't act like you're not feeling it, too..."

"This is ridiculous." Gabe glanced at the night sky and scrubbed a hand across his face.

"You're the one who wanted to talk."

"Yeah, well, maybe I was wrong. Maybe the time for talking is over."

He did a hasty scan of the area then pulled Devin into a nearby doorway, trapping her there with his body. "Ask me again."

A hot flush spread across her face. "Ask you what?"

"What you asked in the bar." He leaned in and rested his forehead against hers. "About going back to your place."

So he was serious. They were really doing this.

Hot damn.

"Do you want to go back to my place?" *Bad idea.* She was supposed to be putting out the fire smoldering between them. Not dousing it with gasoline.

But what a lovely way to burn...

Dear Reader,

It's hard to believe this is my second crack at a Dear Reader letter. I'm thrilled to share book two of the Art of Seduction series with you.

Each of the books in this series has the arts as a backdrop. In *Triple Threat* it's theater; in *Triple Time* it's the fine arts. Devin Padilla is a tattoo artist/bartender who paints on the sly. Her life's been tough, and the thing she wants most is to find her brother, separated from her in foster care. But all she's hit are dead ends.

Assistant district attorney Gabe Nelson has his life planned. But when his would-be fiancée and his boss insinuate that he's duller than dirt, he starts to have doubts. Then Devin strolls in, all tattoos and piercings and take-no-prisoners attitude. She might need help, but she's no damsel in distress. When she learns Gabe's running for the top spot in the DA's office, she offers him a deal: she'll help him loosen up so he can win his retiring boss's endorsement if he helps find her brother.

Devin and Gabe were a blast to introduce in *Triple Threat*, and I loved telling their story in *Triple Time*. Theirs is a journey of opposites fighting their attraction every step of the way. I hope you have as much fun following it as I did writing it.

And in December you'll get to meet Gabe's twin sister, Ivy, when she returns to Stockton and faces her first and only love—her brother's best friend, Cade Hardesty.

Until then,

Regina

Regina Kyle

Triple Time

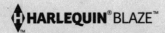
HARLEQUIN® BLAZE™

Recycling programs
for this product may
not exist in your area.

ISBN-13: 978-0-373-79854-4

Triple Time

Copyright © 2015 by Denise Smoker

Printed in U.S.A.

A12006 449798

Regina Kyle knew she was destined to be an author when she won a writing contest at age eight with a touching tale about a squirrel and a nut pie. By day, she writes dry legal briefs, representing the state in criminal appeals. At night, she writes steamy romance with heart and humor. A lover of all things theatrical, Regina lives on the Connecticut shoreline with her husband, teenage daughter and two melodramatic cats. When she's not writing, she's most likely singing, reading, cooking or watching bad reality television. She loves hearing from readers. You can find her on Facebook at facebook.com/reginakyleauthor, follow her on Twitter @Regina_Kyle1, or sign up for her newsletter at reginakyle.com.

Books by Regina Kyle

HARLEQUIN BLAZE

The Art of Seduction

Triple Threat

To get the inside scoop on Harlequin Blaze and its talented writers, be sure to check out blazeauthors.com.

All backlist available in ebook format.

Visit the Author Profile page at Harlequin.com for more titles.

For Ernie, who never says no to my crazy ideas, even the ones hatched in the midst of a midlife crisis. And Marissa, who showed me how to reach for my dream by grabbing hers with both hands and never letting go. They both put up with more than their fair share of plotting disguised as incoherent muttering, deadline-induced panic, dirty laundry and take-out dinners.

And I love them for it.

1

BY THE TIME the Perfect Moment arrived for Gabe Nelson to pop the question, his tongue felt like lead, too thick for the elaborate script he'd written in his head. So he decided to keep it simple.

"Will you marry me?"

Gabe held his breath as he got down on one knee and snapped open the robin's-egg-blue box. Inside a flawless two-carat, emerald-cut diamond sparkled, catching the light from the crystal chandeliers dotting New York City's famous Rainbow Room restaurant.

"I...I don't know what to say." Kara Humphries, Gabe's girlfriend for the past six months, stared at the ring as if it were a two-headed hydra instead of a precious gem.

Not exactly the reaction he'd been hoping for.

He swallowed. Hard. His mind whirred through plans B, C and D. She hadn't exactly said no. There had to be some way to persuade her to accept his proposal.

"Say yes." Gabe took one of her perfectly manicured hands and brought it to his lips, kissing her palm for extra effect. Hell, he hadn't served four years in the Navy JAG corps, then clawed his way to the top spot in the Manhattan DA's Special Victims Bureau by giving up without a fight.

She pulled her hand away and tucked it under the napkin in her lap. "I'm sorry, Gabe. You're a great guy. Really. Any woman would be lucky to have you. But…"

Ouch. Direct hit. He stood and slunk back into his seat. With sweaty hands, he palmed the ring box, snapped it shut and stuffed it into the inside pocket of his suit jacket. He could feel his heart pounding under the cool cotton of his dress shirt. "Just not this woman, right? It's not me, it's you. Isn't that how the saying goes?"

"Actually…" She looked down, her hands fiddling with her napkin. After a moment that seemed as long as the wait for his results on the bar exam, her gaze rose to meet his. "It is you. And me."

"What's that supposed to mean?" He tried not to sound hurt, but it wasn't easy. He wasn't used to setting his mind on something and not seeing it through. As far he was concerned, this engagement wasn't any different from negotiating a plea bargain. He and Kara belonged together.

He just had to seal the deal.

She lifted a hand to brush an imaginary lock of her always impeccable ash-blond hair from her cheek, then let it flutter back to her lap. "We both like jazz. The symphony. Sailing. Fine wine."

"Exactly." He raised his glass of 1998 Veuve Clicquot—the two-hundred-dollar bottle of champagne he'd specially chosen to toast their engagement—and took a sip, eyeing her over the rim with a half smile. A kernel of hope settled in his chest and he sat a little straighter. She was making his point for him. "It's called compatibility. I fail to see the problem."

"That *is* the problem." Her voice broke and she took a deep breath. "There's no spark between us. I adore you, Gabe, and I hope we stay friends. But I planned to tell you tonight that I think we should stop seeing each other. We're too much alike. I need someone who'll challenge me, broaden my horizons, introduce me to new things."

He leaned in and studied her intently, his initial shock slowly receding. A mix of determination and curiosity took its place.

"I can introduce you to new things." Why not? She wanted adventure, he'd give her adventure. He could be as fun and spontaneous as the next guy. If he had enough time to prepare.

"Oh, Gabe. You're sweet. But your idea of a new thing is having red wine with fish instead of white. I'm talking about really living life. Taking chances. Not the same old boring stuff we always do."

His jaw tightened and he locked his fingers together. "So I'm boring?"

"Not exactly. Just predictable." She stood, placed her napkin on her plate and smoothed down her skirt. "I'm sorry, Gabe. I wanted it to work. Really, I did. But I can't pretend anymore, trying to make myself feel something that's not there. Someday you'll meet the right woman. I'm just not her."

She made her way through the restaurant, a chorus of whispers in her wake. An occupational hazard of being the daughter of a senator and one of New York's most prominent—and wealthy—philanthropists.

He sat alone and uncomfortable, staring into his plate of shrimp scampi. What the hell had just happened? He had planned everything so perfectly. Perfect place. Perfect time. Perfect woman.

Or so he'd thought.

He was thirty years old, for Christ's sake. He wanted a wife. Kids before he was too old to enjoy them. Of all the women he'd dated—and he was no John Mayer, but he'd gone out with his fair share—Kara was the only one he could see in his life for the long haul. A real partner in every way, beside him at rallies and fundraisers. Entertaining guests, or relaxing together at the end of a long,

stressful day, reading or listening to John Coltrane on his
state-of-the-art sound system. Okay, so they weren't burning up the sheets just yet. That would come in time. Right?

But she'd said no. Said he was too predictable. Which,
in his book, meant boring, no matter how she tried to
sugarcoat it.

"Your check, sir."

Gabe looked up at the waiter's sheepish expression.
He'd clearly witnessed the whole unfortunate scene.

"Here." Gabe took the leather holder in the waiter's outstretched hand, stuck his credit card inside without even
looking at the bill and handed it back to him.

The waiter left, leaving Gabe alone. Again. He shifted
in his seat and glanced around the dining room, catching the sympathetic looks of several patrons who quickly
averted their eyes, like the waiter, obviously privy to his
humiliation.

His very public humiliation.

Not soon enough, the waiter came back with Gabe's
credit card. With a gruff "Thanks," Gabe scrawled his
signature, downed the rest of his champagne and strode
through the restaurant, slipping out into the New York
night.

His apartment was only a few blocks south, but he
headed in the other direction, toward Central Park. Not
the best place to be at night, especially a night like this
one. Ripe. Sweltering. Sure to lure out every crazy without
air-conditioning. But he wasn't ready to go home yet. He
needed to breathe, to think, and nothing cleared his head
like a run in the park. Tonight his suit meant he'd have to
settle for a brisk walk, even if it meant he'd be covered
in sweat by the time he got to his apartment downtown.

He circled the sailboat pond, trying to figure out why
he felt more numb than crushed by Kara's refusal, when a

high-pitched voice from behind the boathouse froze him in his Ferragamo shoes.

"Get your fucking hands off me, or I'll knee your balls right through the roof of your goddamned mouth."

Gabe did a one-eighty and sprinted toward the sound.

A woman stood with her back to him, fists clenched. Her attacker lay curled at her feet, wheezing for air.

"No means no, asshole."

The guy let out a muffled moan and she bent over him, making her short skirt ride even higher up her toned thighs. Her fishnet stockings covered her long legs, disappearing midcalf into a pair of hot-pink Doc Martens.

"Okay, okay. You made your point. You didn't have to kick me so hard. Frigid bitch."

Gabe stepped out of the shadow of the boathouse. "Watch your mouth. And don't move a damn muscle. I'm calling the police." He pulled out his cell phone and started to dial.

"No cops. Please." The woman held out an arm as if to stop him, and Gabe caught a glimpse of a tattoo on her shoulder. A distinctive, familiar tattoo of some sort of forest fairy. "Freddie just got a little overeager. But I set him straight." She prodded him with one boot, eliciting another moan. "Didn't I, Freddie?"

Gabe's stomach clenched. "Devin?"

She pivoted slowly, her eyes widening and her mouth falling open in recognition.

"Shit."

OF ALL THE white knights in New York City, why did Gabe Nelson have to be the one to ride to her rescue?

Devin Padilla stared at her best friend's brother and swore again.

"It's nice to see you, too."

She crossed her arms. "What are you doing here?"

"Heading home. Same as you should be." Disapproval dripped from his voice as he eyeballed her, frowning no doubt at her outfit of choice. Sure, the lacy camisole clung a little too tightly to her 36Ds and her short skirt showed off her J. Lo booty. But she was a bartender, for Christ's sake, not an astrophysicist. How was she supposed to earn enough tips to support herself and set something aside for Victor if—no, *when*—she found him, if she didn't give her customers something to look at on top of her witty repartee.

"Isn't that dive you work at downtown?"

"It's not a dive. And yes, it is. Sometimes I pull extra shifts for a friend at The Mark." She never said no to extra cash, and she always raked it in at the Upper East Side hotel bar.

"Hello?" a voice interrupted from the pavement. "Injured man down here."

"Get up, Freddie. You're not hurt. I barely touched you."

"You know this guy?" Gabe asked.

"He's one of my regulars. Said he'd take me to the subway." She glared down at him, hands on her hips. Just another one in a long line of losers that had hit on her in the past six months. It was like she was wearing a sign that said *Attention all guys. Are you mentally stable? Gainfully employed? Reasonably attractive? Then keep away.* "The subway, Freddie. Not to heaven against a slimy park viaduct."

Freddie struggled to his knees. "It's not my fault. You've been giving me mixed signals for months."

"Mixed signals?" She raised one Doc Marten and aimed it at him, making him flinch before she broke off and scuffed the ground in front of him. He scuttled back like a frightened crab and she couldn't help but scoff. "How's that for a mixed signal, dirtbag?"

Gabe put a hand on her shoulder. "You're relieved from duty, Freddie. I'll see the lady home."

"Like hell you will." Devin shook off his hand. No way she was spending one minute more than necessary with Dudley Do-Right. No matter how dead sexy he was. "The subway's two blocks from here. I can make it just fine on my own."

"I'm sure you can. But a gentleman always makes sure his date arrives home safely." Gabe tugged off his suit jacket and wrapped it around Devin's shoulders, shielding them—and the breasts barely concealed by her skimpy top—from Freddie's prying eyes. "Isn't that right, Freddie?"

"I'm not your date." Devin's gaze ping-ponged from one man to the other. "Either of you."

"Humor me." Gabe's hand held steady against the small of her back. The shivers she hadn't noticed subsided, tempting her to succumb to the warm, reassuring feeling of a good man's touch.

His touch.

"Have it your way." Freddie stood and backed away slowly. "But I'm telling you, man, the chick is trouble."

Devin started for him but Gabe held her back, and damn if his touch didn't make her quiver all over again. What was it about Holly's stuffed-shirt brother that got her engine revving faster than a dirt bike at the X Games?

It couldn't be the banging body she was pretty sure he hid under all those designer suits—broad shoulders that led to an equally broad chest, narrow waist, lean hips and long, strong legs. Or his stormy, gray eyes, intense and mysterious, never revealing what was going on behind them. And it sure as hell wasn't his lips, full, firm and just right for hours of sensuous kissing.

"That's a chance I'll have to take." Gabe slid his hand to her elbow, leaving a trail of goose bumps in its wake.

"It's your funeral," Freddie tossed over his shoulder as he fled into the darkness.

"Asshole." Devin watched him disappear then turned to Gabe. "I appreciate your help…"

"But you're fine. Yeah. Got it."

She shook off his jacket, thrust it at him and headed for the subway. She hadn't gone three steps when he caught up with her. "Nice try, but you're not getting rid of me that easily. I meant what I said. I'm taking you home."

His eyes sparked with something. Anger? Frustration? Devin's insides tingled in response. Maybe letting him take her home wasn't such a bad idea. Then he could take her against the living room wall. And on the kitchen counter. And in the…

"Besides, my sister would kill me if she found out I left you alone in Central Park in the middle of the night."

Right. His sister. Duty, not fantasy. Thanks for the verbal equivalent of a cold shower.

"Fine," she huffed. "But we're taking a cab. Your treat."

"My pleasure."

He took her arm, propelling her toward Fifth Avenue, where he hailed a cab. Hustling her inside, he gave the cabby her address, one he knew well since, until recently, his sister had lived in the apartment directly below Devin's.

"How is Holly?" she asked to break the awkward silence that descended once the cab pulled into traffic. "I haven't talked to her in almost a month. Since she and Nick left for Istanbul."

"She loves it there." Gabe loosened his tie and unbuttoned the first couple of buttons on his impeccably pressed white cotton dress shirt, revealing a triangle of fine dark chest hair. "But my parents are worried sick about her. I can't believe her doctor let her travel in her condition."

Devin swallowed hard and turned to stare out the window. She'd tattooed her share of gorgeous, muscle-bound men and hadn't so much as blinked. But one glimpse of Mr. GQ's freaking chest hair and she was practically hyperventilating.

Pathetic.

"News flash," Devin said when she could finally breathe again. "Holly's not due for like five months. Women in her *condition* travel all the time. And Nick added an ob-gyn and a nurse to their entourage."

With his money, he could have a fully staffed maternity ward on set if he wanted to. And she had no doubt he would if shooting on his latest Trent Savage pic went longer than expected. She'd never seen a couple as devoted to each other as Nick and Holly. It was almost enough to make her forget what a fucking farce love could be.

Almost.

They lapsed back into silence. Devin focused on the blurred buildings speeding by outside the grimy window. But no matter how hard she tried, she couldn't ignore Gabe, sitting only inches away. His thigh brushing hers when he shifted. The scent of his cologne—citrusy, with a hint of cedar—teasing her senses.

Majorly pathetic.

"Can I ask you something?" His words tumbled out, like he was afraid if he didn't say them at light speed, they wouldn't come out at all.

"Uh, sure." She turned to him with a shrug. "I guess so."

"Would you say I'm…" He raked a hand through his close-cropped, chestnut hair. "Do you think I'm, well, boring?"

Devin almost choked. Boring? Seriously? Of all the words in the English language, boring was just about the last one she'd choose to describe Gabe Nelson. A little straitlaced, maybe. Serious. Panty-meltingly hot. But boring?

Hell, no.

She opened her mouth to answer but Gabe waved her off. "Never mind. Your hesitation speaks volumes."

His shoulders stiffened and he turned his back to her to stare out his window.

Shit. What was it about this guy that always made her say the wrong thing, do the wrong thing? It was as if she was a tongue-tied teenage girl with a crush on her best friend's hunky, totally hands-off younger brother.

Which was exactly what she was. Except for the teenage part.

Before she could figure out a way to straighten him out while salvaging her pride, they pulled up outside her apartment building and Gabe hopped out of the cab, holding the door for her.

"Keep the meter running," he instructed the cabbie. "I'll be right back."

She brushed past him, ignoring his outstretched hand, and he followed her up the steps to the main door.

"Thanks," she said, digging in her purse for her key. Where the hell was it? All she wanted was to get inside, change into sweats, scarf down a pint of Ben & Jerry's Coffee Toffee Bar Crunch and forget this whole humiliating night. "Look, about what you asked earlier, in the cab. You're not boring. A little repressed, maybe."

"Repressed?"

"You know. Old-fashioned. Conservative."

She let out a yelp as Gabe spun her around, pressing her against the door with his hips. "How's this for conservative?"

"This" was his hands on her shoulders, his lips crushing hers. After a moment of shock, her body responded to him. Her purse slipped from her fingers, her keys forgotten, and her arms came up to circle his neck. Her hands tangled in his hair, holding him tight. Her lips parted and he didn't waste any time in taking advantage, stealing his tongue into the opening and sweeping it across her lower lip.

Hot flipping damn. She was right about those lips of his. She could kiss them for hours. Days, even. And that naughty tongue…

She mentally struck straightlaced off her list of adjectives for him.

Not to be outdone, she met him lick for lick, running her tongue over his teeth and into the corners of his mouth. With a moan, he nudged her legs apart with his knee and moved between them. She could feel his rock-hard thigh pressing against her core.

She was ready to hook one leg around his hip and grind against him like a stripper on a pole when he broke off the kiss as abruptly as he'd started it.

"Christ, Devin, I'm…"

She pushed against his chest, resisting the temptation to grab his designer shirt in her fists and pull him back to her. "If you say you're sorry, I'll…"

He backed away, thrusting his hands in his pockets. "Knee my balls right through the roof of my goddamned mouth?"

"Something like that."

"Then I'll just say good-night." One corner of his mouth curled into a half smile. "And sweet dreams."

She slumped against the door, needing something to keep her vertical, as he climbed into the cab and drove away. Only when the taillights disappeared from view did she let herself slink to the ground, fumbling for her purse in disbelief.

Dudley Do-Right had done what no man had done before.

He'd left her wanting more.

2

"Hey, Nelson. Boss wants to see you."

"In a sec." Gabe's fingers flew over the keyboard, his eyes never straying from the computer screen. "I'm almost done with this motion."

"Boss says now."

Gabe looked up at his second-in-command, Jack Kentfield. "What gives?"

Jack lifted a shoulder. "Who knows? But you're wanted on the seventh floor ASAP."

"Great." Gabe hit Save, closed the document and pushed away from his desk. Being summoned to the penthouse could only mean one of two things. Either he'd screwed up and was going to have his ass handed to him or he'd pleased the powers that be and was getting a commendation.

He wasn't in the mood for either.

"Good luck," Jack called after him as he headed for the elevator. "If you're not back in ten I'll send up a search party. Or start a memorial fund."

"Make sure you hit up Tim in elder abuse." The elevator doors opened and Gabe stepped in. "He owes me twenty bucks."

The doors slid shut, leaving Gabe alone to wonder which fate awaited him upstairs. He couldn't think of anything he'd done to warrant an ass reaming. Although, to be honest, his mind hadn't totally been on his work since that night with Devin in the park last week. And on her doorstep.

Their kiss had been nothing short of explosive. Way more intense than anything he'd experienced before. He prided himself on his control. His ability to think before acting. All that had gone the way of the cassette tape when Devin surrendered to him, her soft lips parting under his, her full, warm curves molding to him.

A stirring below his belt buckle made him shake his head and silently scold himself. *Down, boy. Big meeting coming up. Think clean thoughts. Mom. Apple pie. A busload of nuns on their way to a prayer meeting.*

Gabe squeezed his eyes shut. He'd been a selfish, impulsive bastard to kiss her, but at least one good thing had come of it. Now he understood why Kara's rejection had left him more numb than hurt. He'd been an idiot, proposing to her for all the wrong reasons. Thinking he could choose a life mate based on shared interests and political expediency. Thinking passion would come later and build slowly, like a roller coaster climbing that first hill.

It wouldn't. And it wouldn't have been fair to her. Or him.

With a *ding*, the elevator doors opened and Gabe stepped into the inner sanctum of Manhattan District Attorney Thaddeus Holcomb. Teddy to his friends. Mr. Holcomb to his underlings at One Hogan Place.

"Gabe." Doris, Mr. Holcomb's secretary from what seemed like the dawn of time, beckoned him closer with a wrinkled finger. "He's waiting for you."

She ushered him into an office three times the size of his own. Instead of a regulation-issue gunmetal gray desk like Gabe's, the current district attorney sat behind a massive oak table. Matching bookshelves lined the walls, bright blue statute books and thick legal treatises artfully arranged alongside plaques, trophies and the occasional family photo.

"You wanted to see me?" Gabe took a seat in one of the two leather armchairs in front of the table.

Holcomb closed the file he'd been reading. "Nice work on Patterson. Convincing Judge Morrison to let in the defendant's statement."

"Thanks." Gabe relaxed into the soft leather. Looked like it was going to be door number two.

"Any word on sentencing?"

"It's scheduled for next Thursday."

"Good. Keep me posted."

Holcomb cleared his throat. Gabe steeled himself. Now came the real reason for their little tête-à-tête. Holcomb pushed the file across the table. "The police made an arrest in the Park Avenue homicide case last night."

Gabe nodded. It'd been all over the morning news. A handyman was accused of sexually assaulting and murdering an eighty-five-year-old woman and her live-in nurse. A witness saw him leaving their apartment shortly before the bodies were discovered. "He'll be arraigned tomorrow. Kentfield's handling it."

Holcomb shook his head. "I want you on this case. It's a publicity magnet."

Gabe folded his arms across his chest and frowned. Jack might be a bit of a prick, but he could handle the press as well as anyone. There had to be more to this than the boss was letting on. "What aren't you telling me?"

"Nothing." Holcomb shrugged, his innocent expression making Gabe even more convinced the DA had a secret agenda. "You're my best prosecutor. You're taking this one. End of story."

Gabe picked up the file and stood. He knew when to press his luck and when to walk away. "No problem."

"I'm not done yet." Holcomb motioned for Gabe to sit

back down, so he did. "There's another matter we have to discuss."

"Is there a problem?" Gabe's frown deepened.

"I understand you're thinking about running for this position when I retire next year."

"Yes, sir." Running for public office was the next logical step in Gabe's career plan. First district attorney, then the state legislature and maybe even Congress. He figured he'd have to wait a few years before starting down that road. But Holcomb's announcement that he wouldn't run for a third term had sped up Gabe's timeline a bit.

"I expect you'll want my endorsement."

"I was hoping." Holcomb just admitted Gabe was his best prosecutor. That had to count for something.

"You're an excellent lawyer, Gabe. The youngest man ever to head Special Victims." Holcomb tilted his chair back, and Gabe's heart rate kicked up a notch. This was it. Holcomb was going to give him his thumbs up. And with his backing, Gabe would be the front runner for DA.

"But I can't endorse you."

Wait, what?

The "thank you" he'd been about to utter stuck in his throat. Gabe barely suppressed a cough. "I don't understand."

"There's more to being district attorney than trying cases." Holcomb crossed one ankle over his knee. "You're the face of the division. The people's representative."

"And you don't think I'm ready for that?"

Holcomb twisted the gold signet ring he always wore on his right pinkie finger. "I don't think the people of Manhattan are ready for you."

"What's that mean?" Gabe rubbed the back of his neck. He'd been crusading for justice ever since fourth grade, when he'd begged to be appointed hall monitor so he could help stop the bullying that went on behind the teachers' backs. Now the feeling of his well-orchestrated future slipping away washed over him like fog. Cold. Damp. Foreboding.

"Let me put it to you this way." Holcomb tented his fingers under his chin. "Remember the grand opening of the Family Justice Center?"

Gabe shuddered.

As if he could forget it.

The ceremony had been the one and only time Holcomb had asked Gabe to stand in for him. And it was a disaster from beginning to end. All his courtroom skills had deserted him. He'd flubbed the deputy mayor's name, accidentally insulted the governor's wife and dropped the cartoonishly large scissors trying to cut the damned ribbon.

But that wasn't even the worst of it. No, the worst came later, at the reception, where he had to mix and mingle. Make small talk. Be charming.

He'd tried. But the harder he did, the more awkward the conversations became. He was about as charming as a cardboard box. He'd ended up leaving early, claiming he had to prepare for a trial the next day.

He could face a panel of black-robed Supreme Court justices. A jury of his peers. But put him in a room and make him talk to strangers one-on-one?

Crash and burn.

"Stick to your comfort zone." Holcomb spun his chair around to reach for something on the credenza behind him, dismissing Gabe. "Shaking hands and kissing babies isn't your forte. And it's a job requirement for district attorney."

"I can learn," Gabe insisted. "Give me a chance."

Holcomb twirled back around to face him, considering him through narrowed eyes. "Tell you what. The Feast of San Gennaro is in a few weeks."

"Right." Everyone knew that. The Italian street fair was one of New York City's biggest and most popular events.

"I make a point to attend every year. Come with me, prove you can fit in with the crowd, and I'll reconsider."

"Fit in?"

"Meet people. Talk to them. Show me you can convince them to vote for you."

"It's a deal."

Gabe rose, and Holcomb followed suit, extending his hand. "Good luck."

"Thanks." He was going to need it. Because he had less than a month to learn how to "fit in" with the masses who populated the festival. And no freaking clue how he was going to do it.

"NOT IN SERVICE my ass." Devin punched the End Call button on her cell phone.

Her boss and mentor, Leo Zambrano, looked up from the triceps he was tattooing and smirked. "You realize you're talking to an automated message, right?"

"That low-life, rat bastard PI's disconnected his phone." She circled her station at Ink the Heights, the Washington Heights tattoo parlor where she'd worked since she was eighteen and Leo had caught her camped out in the storeroom. Instead of the boot, he gave her an apprenticeship, and he put up with her even on days like today. It was a damned good thing her next customer was running late. In this mood, she might accidentally stab him with a needle.

"The one Manny referred you to?" Leo wiped a spot of blood from his customer's arm with a paper towel and studied his handiwork. The dark outline of a phoenix rising from the rubble of the Twin Towers stood out against Hector's olive skin. "His cousin's friend's sister's boyfriend, or something?"

"Yep. The jackass totally screwed me. Took my thousand-dollar retainer, told me he was on the trail of a hot lead then disappeared." She paced between her station and Leo's, needing some way to work off her anxiety short of tipping over the autoclave and dumping sterile instruments all over the floor.

"Can't Manny track him down?" Their errand boy knew everything about everyone in the Heights.

Devin shook her head. "He tried. Says the guy dumped his cousin's friend's whatever three days ago and hopped a plane to Miami. Probably his first stop on his way to San Juan. How am I going to find Victor now? All I hit on my own was dead ends. And I can't afford to pay anyone else. Hell, it took me months to scrape up that thousand."

She balled her hands into fists. It wasn't just the money that got to her, although losing a grand sucked big time. It was that for the first time in years she'd felt like she was getting close to finding her brother, only to have that hope snatched away, leaving her empty, depressed and mad as hell at the snatcher.

Then there was the article she'd read a few weeks ago in the *Times* about a group home for mentally disabled adults in the Bronx that was shut down after reporters for one of the local news programs found residents being verbally abused, pushed, kicked, starved and even spat on. What if Victor was in a place like that? "I swear, if that little pissant shows his face in this neighborhood again I'll…"

"Kick him in the balls?" Leo smirked and went back to tattooing. "Like you did to Fast Fingers Freddie?"

"Worse. More like rip them off and shove them down his lying throat."

"I could loan you—"

"No." She stopped pacing to stare him down. "I'm not taking your money. Haven't you rescued me enough?"

"You're the one bailing me out these days. You're good.

Better than good. I keep expecting you to toss me for one of those fancy places near your apartment downtown."

She shrugged. "What can I say? I have a fondness for aging *bobos* with a hero complex."

"And I'm partial to smart-mouthed *muchachas* who insist on doing things their own way." Leo set down his needle, took another swipe at the tattoo with the paper towel, and covered it with a bandage. "That's it for today, Hector. We'll start on the shading next week. Same time."

"Thanks, man." Hector flung a few bills onto the counter on his way out. "See you in seven."

Leo peeled off his gloves, threw them into the trash can reserved for medical waste and crossed to the Keurig machine on the other side of the room. He held up a K-Cup. "Want one?"

"No, thanks." Devin checked the clock above the sink. Three twenty-five. Almost half an hour past her client's appointment time. Probably another case of cold feet. "I'm wound up enough already."

Leo shrugged and started his cup brewing. "So you won't take my money. What's next? The police?"

Devin choked out a laugh. "What's the point? The scumbag's long gone, and the cops aren't going to chase after him for a measly thousand bucks."

"How about Holly's brother?" The machine stopped gurgling, and he removed his mug, taking a long, slow sip of the dark roast. "Doesn't he work for the DA's office?"

"Gabe?" She turned her back to Leo, emptied the autoclave and tossed in a handful of fresh tools to be sterilized, glad for the excuse to hide her reddening face. "What about him?"

"He saved your sorry ass when you ran into him last week. Maybe he can help again."

Ran into him. That was a major understatement. But she'd only told Leo that Gabe had found her in Central

Park and taken her home. And she wouldn't have even told him that if he hadn't asked about the bruises on her upper arms from where that fuckup Freddie had grabbed her.

"My ass is not sorry, and he did not save it." She released her hair from its messy ponytail, gathered it up again and secured it with the scrunchie she held in her teeth. "I took care of myself. And Freddie. Mr. Clean didn't know when to leave well enough alone."

"Well, Mr. Clean looks like your best bet to get your money back. Maybe even find Victor."

Devin stopped, her hand on the pressure switch of the autoclave. She knew she'd never get the cash back. But it hadn't occurred to her that Gabe could help find her brother. "How so?"

Leo lifted one shoulder and sipped his coffee. "He's in Special Victims, right? He must know people in Child Services."

Damn. Why hadn't she thought of that before?

Only one problem. It would mean indebting herself to the man she wanted to jump every time she got within ten feet of him. The one she should be avoiding like day old *alcapurrias*.

Her best friend's off-limits, way-out-of-her-league baby brother.

It wasn't just his relationship to Holly that made Gabe untouchable. It didn't take a Rhodes Scholar to figure out he was built for commitment. Marriage. Two point five kids. A minimansion in Scarsdale. The whole nine yards.

And Devin…wasn't.

She flipped the switch on the autoclave and sighed, her breath stirring the loose strands that had already escaped her ponytail.

"I know that look." Leo leaned against the counter, setting his mug down behind him. Above his shoulder, framed photos of her work—and his—hung against the backdrop of the cheery lemon-yellow wall, constant reminders of how far she'd come since that fateful day when Leo had taken her in off the street. But not far enough for a smart, sophisticated guy like Gabe. "It's your I-am-an-island look. The one you give when you want to scare everyone off and convince them you can go it alone."

Sure. Fine. Let's run with that.

"There's no shame in relying on your friends every once in a while, *hermanita*." He crossed to her and tugged her ponytail. "That's what we're here for."

She softened at the use of his nickname for her. *Little sister.* "I know. I'm just…"

"Not used to depending on anyone. I get that. But this is Victor we're talking about. Your brother. Who you haven't seen in, what, twelve years?"

She winced, remembering their last minutes together. Her shaking with rage, screaming obscenities at the social worker who had dragged Victor away. Him clutching his favorite stuffed animal, a ratty armadillo, his sweet face wet with tears. Both of them scared shitless. "More like fifteen."

"That's fifteen years too long." The bells hanging over the top of the door tinkled and he went to the sink to scrub his hands, preparing for their new arrival. "If you won't take my money, at least promise you'll think about calling Gabe."

Devin's stomach sank at the thought of facing Gabe again, but that was nothing compared to the way it pitched and rolled when she considered the alternative. Victor, stuck in a house of horrors like the one she'd read about it the paper.

"All right. You win." As usual. She started toward the

front of the shop to greet Leo's next customer. "I'll think about it."

What the hell, she thought as she pasted on a smile. It wasn't as if she could stop thinking about Gabe anyway.

3

PINSTRIPED SUITS. Pencil skirts. Pocket squares.

She was surrounded by yuppies.

They should post warning signs. Caution: Smart Phones at Work.

Devin slowed her steps as she neared One Hogan Place, home of the New York County District Attorney's Office. She glanced down at her outfit. She'd gone as conservatively as she could, given the limits of her wardrobe—a plain, black T-shirt, khaki cargo pants and black Doc Martens. Clean. Neat. Well-pressed. But compared to the Wall Street types, she looked like a refugee from a doomsday cult.

"Move it or lose it, honey." One of the pinstripe-suited businessmen shoved past her, knocking her oversize bag off her shoulder, no doubt late for some all-important meeting.

"Thanks, asshole." She managed to pick up her bag, narrowly missing being trampled by a candy-apple-red stiletto.

Now she remembered why she hated the financial district.

Her Greenwich Village neighborhood, and even the Heights, had a cool, edgy vibe. Sure, people there worked hard. But they knew how to play, too. Here, everything was go-go-go 24/7. Even play was work. Gotta swim more laps than the next guy. Beat him at racquetball. Be the best on the golf course. Or whatever these uptight over-achievers did in the name of relaxation.

Yet another reminder of why she and Gabe would be a match made in purgatory. Okay, so the guy kissed like a porn star. But aside from that, he needed some serious help in the recreation department. Probably wouldn't know fun if it jumped out of his briefcase and bit him in the oh-so-delectable ass. Certainly not her kind of fun.

And after a lifetime of struggling, Devin was all about fun.

But not now. She was here for one reason and one reason only.

To find Victor.

She pushed open the ornate brass door. The cool, conditioned air blasted her in the face as she crossed the lobby to the concierge. "District Attorney's Office?"

"Reception's on the third floor." He gestured toward the elevators behind him.

"Thanks."

Her boots echoed on the marble tile, and she ignored the stares of the preppy elite as she jabbed at the elevator button. She breathed a relieved sigh when the doors slid open and she could escape into the quiet of the thankfully empty car.

She slumped against the wall, watching the indicator on the ancient elevator inch its way from one to three. For the thousandth time, she mentally rehearsed her speech.

Hey, Gabe. Thanks for rescuing me in the park last week. Even though I really didn't need rescuing. Can I ask you for one more teeny, tiny favor? Help find my brother who got separated from me in foster care when I was thirteen.

Ugh. It didn't sound any better in her head than it had

in the living/bedroom of her tiny studio apartment. But she was running out of options.

Devin groaned. She hated, hated, hated asking for help. Especially when she didn't have anything to offer in return. Well, nothing a guy like Gabe would want, anyway.

She ran through a few more variations of her speech but wasn't any closer to knowing what she would say when the doors opened.

"Can I help you?" A pretty, way-too-pert receptionist greeted Devin when she stepped off the elevator.

"I'm here to see Gabe Nelson."

"Do you have an appointment?" She clicked a few buttons on her desktop computer. "I don't see anything on his schedule until after lunch."

"Um, no. Not exactly." Devin tugged self-consciously on her T-shirt. "I'm a friend of the family."

A scowl creased the receptionist's forehead. "Let me see what I can do. Who should I tell him is here?"

"Devin."

"Just Devin?" She raised a skeptical eyebrow.

Devin hitched her bag up on her shoulder and crossed her arms. "He'll know who it is."

The receptionist waved her over to a line of chairs against the wall, and Devin sat while the woman spoke in low tones into the telephone. A few minutes later, Gabe rounded the corner, the confused expression on his face not detracting one damned bit from his hotness. In a charcoal-gray suit, pale blue dress shirt and burgundy tie, his dark-framed glasses made him look like a grown up, uber-sexy Harry Potter.

"Devin. What brings you here? Everything okay?"

She stood and wiped her damp hands on her cargo pants. "Can we talk in private?" The last thing she needed was the entire office hearing her sob story. Bad enough she had to tell Gabe.

"Sure." He led her past the receptionist and down a narrow corridor to his office. It was Spartan but functional. Government-issue desk. Two guest chairs. Filing cabinets along the walls with an array of photos. She spotted Holly, Gabe's parents, his younger sister, Noelle, and what she assumed was Ivy, his twin, a fashion photographer who was always off on some shoot or another. One big, smiling, happy family. Something she sure as hell never had.

He crossed to a minifridge in the corner, opened it and held up a plastic bottle. "Want a water? Or I can have Stephanie get you some coffee?"

"Water's fine, thanks," she croaked. Nerves were strange things. Moistening her palms. Drying her throat.

He handed her the bottle, took one for himself and sat behind the desk, motioning for her to do the same in one of the guest chairs opposite him. "I take it this isn't a social call."

He cracked open his water bottle, tipped his head back and took a long chug. His Adam's apple bobbed, and she crossed her legs to control the tingling at her core.

Fan-fucking-tastic. First chest hair. Now this. What would set her off next? His toenails?

"I brought you something." She dug into her handbag. Starting with a little bribe couldn't hurt. "To say thanks. For the other night."

Gabe tilted his head and gave her a cocky smile.

"The cab ride. Freak." She plunked a Tupperware container onto the desk. "Arroz con pollo. It's homemade."

"You cook?"

She shrugged. "I didn't say whose home."

He laughed, a low, smoky sound that made her insides flutter. "You came all the way downtown to bring me food?"

"You looked a little peaked." She twisted off the cap of her water bottle and sipped, the liquid soothing her throat but doing nothing for her overheated libido. "But if you don't want it, I can take it back."

He slapped a palm on top of the container and slid it toward him. "My mother always told me it's rude to refuse a gift."

Devin looked down at her lap and pretended to be fascinated with her fingernails, hoping it masked the stab of longing at the mention of his mother. All her mother had ever taught her was how to roll a joint and make a mean vodka martini. Like James Bond, shaken, not stirred. Oh, and that nothing—and no one—was forever.

"So." Gabe put the container in the fridge and sat back at his desk, resting his chin on his fist. "Here we are. In private. Are you going to tell me why you're really here?"

She shifted to the edge of her seat and raised her head to meet his gaze. Damn, those storm-cloud eyes were distracting. All dark and distant and moody. She blinked twice to break the spell. "I need your…"

The words stuck in her throat, and she started again. "I need your help to find my brother."

There. That wasn't so bad, was it?

He sat silent and unmoving, the eyes behind his glasses unreadable, the only sound in the room the hum of the minifridge.

No, it wasn't so bad. It was worse.

HOLY SHIT.

She had a brother? And, more importantly, she didn't know where he was?

He'd barely had time to process this information, much less respond, when the door burst open and a slick, blond head popped in.

"Where's the Rasmusson file?"

Only Jack would enter his office without knocking. And only Jack would hone in on Devin like a heat-seeking missile, sidling into the other guest chair and pulling it closer to her.

"I gave it to Stephanie."

So you can beat it. Now.

"Well, hello, gorgeous." Gabe's skin prickled as Jack eyed Devin up and down, lingering a little too long on the tattoo peeking out from the V neck of her T-shirt. Was that a bird? Or a butterfly? Knowing her, it was probably something more provocative, like an arrow with the words "place tongue here."

"Gabe's been holding out on me. I'm Jack Kentfield, the real brains of this operation."

Gabe kicked at the leg of his desk. So much for his psychic powers. Jack wasn't going down without a fight. "Easy, Casanova. How do you know she's not a victim? Or a witness?"

Jack shrugged. "You always meet with them in the conference room."

"Devin Padilla." She held out her hand to him. "I'm friends with Gabe's sister Holly."

"Any friend of Holly is a friend of mine." Jack brought her hand to his lips and kissed it, making Gabe's skin crawl all over again.

"Please. You've met my sister what, twice?"

"Three times, but who's counting?"

"You, apparently." Gabe clenched and unclenched his fists under the cover of his desk, fighting the urge to pop his colleague in the jaw. The only thing that stopped him was Devin, who was looking at Jack as if he was dog doo on the bottom of her boots. "Now, if you don't mind, I was about to take Devin to lunch."

"You were?" She cast a sideways glance at him, her forehead wrinkled.

"Fine, I can take a hint." Jack got up and crossed to the door, throwing one last parting jab over his shoulder.

"You know, Gabe, Holcomb wouldn't think you were such a stick-in-the-mud if he knew you hung out with someone as hot as Devin. Probably endorse you on the spot."

"Endorse you?" Devin leaned in, resting her elbows on her knees. "For what?"

"Never mind." Gabe took off his reading glasses and pinched the bridge of his nose. Damn Jack and his big mouth. Gabe wasn't sure how he'd gotten wind of what had gone down with Holcomb. Gabe sure as hell hadn't told him. But the guy had an uncanny knack for digging up dirt. Suddenly, transferring him to Public Assistance Fraud seemed like a brilliant idea.

Gabe rolled his chair back and stood. "Let's go."

He moved to a coatrack in the corner of the room for his suit jacket and she followed. "You don't have to take me to lunch."

"I don't want to risk any more interruptions." Or give Jack another chance to hit on her.

"I'm not dressed for any place fancy."

"You're perfect for the place I have in mind."

Half an hour later, they were seated across from each other at a table at the Big Apple Burger Bar.

"So." She bit into her burger, closed her eyes and moaned. Her tongue darted out to catch a rivulet of juice but not fast enough to stop it from running down her chin. He gripped the edge of the table, white knuckled, resisting the impulse to wipe—or, better yet, lick—it away. There was something about a woman who enjoyed her food that got him right in the groin.

Devin opened her eyes and dabbed at her mouth with her napkin. "Who's Holcomb? And why does he think you're a stick-in-the-mud?"

"Nice try." Gabe took a bite of his burger. "But we came here to talk about you. And your brother."

She licked her lips and his nether regions stirred again.

"I'll pry it out of you eventually," she said. "You know I will."

"I'm up for the challenge. First tell me about your brother. How can I help?"

"You know people in Child Services, right?"

"Sure." His mind whirred, trying to come up with a reason why Child Services would be involved. Was her brother a minor? Had he run away? Been abused? Abandoned?

She munched on a French fry. "Victor and I were separated in foster care when he was ten and I was thirteen. I haven't seen him since. He's the only family I have left. I filled out an application with the adoption information registry, but…"

"Let me guess. Nothing." Gabe was all too familiar with the registry. It only worked if both parties signed up.

"Yep. I'm not even sure whether he was adopted or stayed in the foster system until he turned eighteen. And the PI I hired was a total bust."

"And now you want me to see what I can find out."

"In a word, yes."

"I'll do what I can." He rubbed a hand across his jaw. He'd figured Devin had had it rough as a kid. He just didn't know how rough. It made him even more eager to help her, if he could. "But if your brother was adopted, and the adoption was sealed…"

"I know. It's an uphill battle. But I have to find him, Gabe. He needs me."

Her hand shook, causing her to drop the fry hovering at her mouth, and Gabe frowned. Something more was going on. Something she wouldn't—or couldn't—tell him. But he wasn't going to press her. Not yet.

He reached across the table and covered her hand with his. A jolt of lust traveled up his arm and through his chest.

Jesus Christ.

What the hell was wrong with him? The woman was distraught, and here he was acting like an overeager teen on his first date.

Gabe gave her hand a quick squeeze and let it go. "I'll do my best. I promise. I'll make some calls tomorrow and let you know what I can dig up."

"Thanks."

She gave him a sad pseudo smile, and they ate in silence for a few minutes.

"Okay," she said finally, plunking her water glass down on the table. "Now that that's settled, I want the whole stick-in-the-mud story."

Damn. He thought she'd forgotten. Should've known better.

"It's not all that exciting."

Kind of like me.

"I'll be the judge of that." She pushed her chair back from the table, stretched out her long legs and crossed her arms, waiting for him to begin.

"All right, but don't blame me if you're bored. Seems to be a common complaint where I'm concerned." He wanted to bite back the words as soon as they were out of his mouth.

"Ah, we're back to that again." She bit her lip, a move only slightly less enticing than licking them. "Look, about that night…"

"You don't have to explain." He reached for his burger.

"Yeah, I do." The tone of her voice—low and somehow desperate, almost urgent—stopped him, and he put the sandwich down. "You're not boring, Gabe. And if Holcomb's telling you that, whoever he is, he's a moron."

"He's my boss. And I'll let him know you feel that way. I'm sure it'll make a big difference." He didn't feel in-

clined to mention that his ex-girlfriend was on the Gabe's-
a-snoozefest bandwagon, too.

"I'm just trying to help. You don't have to get all snarky
on me." She shot up, her chair scraping against the hardwood floor, and reached for her gigantic shoulder bag.

"Devin, wait." He half rose and put a hand on her wrist,
deciding it was better to risk another sexual lightning bolt
than let her leave in a huff, and she hesitated. "I'm sorry.
I guess it's a sore spot with me."

She lowered herself back into the chair, dropping her
purse beside her. "Apology accepted. Now what can I do?"

"Nothing."

She rolled her cornflower-blue eyes, eyes that seemed
so at odds with the rest of her coloring. Pale mocha skin.
Jet black hair. "That's not what your friend Jack seemed
to think."

"He's not my friend." And he wasn't exactly thinking
with the head on his shoulders."

"You want your boss to endorse you for something,
right?" Devin plowed on as if he hadn't even spoken.

Gabe took another swig of root beer and nodded. "District Attorney when he leaves office."

"And he won't because he thinks you're too stuffy."

"In a nutshell."

"So let's unstuff you."

"Unstuff?" His voice rose an octave, and several people turned to stare at them. Could this get any more embarrassing? What was it with him and public humiliation
lately? Maybe he should avoid restaurants altogether for
the foreseeable future.

"Sure." She got up and walked around the table, sur-
veying him from every angle as if he was a prize steer.
He half expected her to pry open his mouth and check his
teeth. "You're good raw material. I can work with that.

And let's face it, I'm probably the least repressed person you know. By a long shot."

Raw material? What did she think this was? Cool Eye for the Uptight Guy?

"Thanks, but no thanks."

"I'm not taking no for an answer." She sat back down across from him, pinning him with those blue eyes, now a deeper almost denim. "Consider it payback. For Victor."

"I haven't found him yet."

"But you agreed to try. That counts for something."

"You're Holly's friend." And, since their kiss, the object of his late-night fantasies. Yet another reason this idea of hers had *train wreck* written all over it. "It's the least I can do. I don't need to be paid back. I'll take my chances at the Feast of San Gennaro."

She tucked her hair behind the ear with four piercings. "What's the feast got to do with it?"

Damn. It was like looking at her made his brain shut down, leaving his mouth to run free. "Holcomb wants me to go with him. Prove I can relate to the 'common man,' whatever that means. Get them to vote for me."

"That gives us…" She pulled her smartphone from her pants pocket and scrolled through her calendar. "Almost six weeks. Plenty of time."

"Time?" He pushed his plate away. "For what?"

She whipped out a notepad and pen from the depths of her bottomless handbag and started scribbling. "For me to loosen you up."

4

"YOU WANT TO take me where?" Gabe crossed his arms and leaned against the doorjamb. It had been three days since Devin had announced her plan to "unstuff" him, and truth be told he hoped she'd forgotten the whole thing. Then she'd shown up at his Tribeca apartment looking like a cast member from *Hair* and said she was taking him to…

"A rave," she repeated, adjusting the fringed tube top she'd paired with a denim miniskirt and white gogo boots. The movement did wonderful things for her breasts. "It's an all-night dance party."

"I know what a rave is." Gabe smirked. "I crawl out from under my rock once in a while." Plus, he had a case a couple of years ago involving a rave.

"Well, come on, then. We're burning midnight."

He looked down at his polo shirt and khakis. Another ten minutes and she would have caught him bare chested and in sweatpants, his usual bedtime attire. "Don't you think I'm a little underdressed?"

She shook her head, her long, dark hair, held off her face by a floral band, rippling. "Anything goes at these things."

He grimaced, remembering his case. Teenagers, illegal substances and slam dancing were a lethal combination. "So I've heard."

"If you're talking about drugs and sex…"

He raised an eyebrow.

She narrowed her eyes at him. "Do you really think I'm so stupid I'd put your job at risk?"

"No, I don't think you're stupid at all." She might not have an Ivy League education like most of his colleagues, but he'd pit her street smarts against their book learning any day.

"Not all raves are dens of iniquity. True rave culture is about peace, unity and respect. It's about expressing yourself in any way you feel comfortable, in a place where you feel no fear, just love and joy from everyone around you."

He snorted. "You sound like a greeting card."

"Very funny. You need to loosen up, and this will get you out of your comfort zone and in touch with younger voters." She tapped one patent-leather toe on the linoleum. "Now quit stalling and let's go."

Busted.

He picked up his keys and wallet from the hall table, stuffed them in his pockets and closed the door. He wasn't pleased that Holcomb seemed to think he needed fixing, but Devin was front and center, ready, willing and able to help him "express himself." Might as well get it over with. "Where exactly are we going?"

She started down the corridor. "A vacant warehouse in the meat-packing district."

He trailed after her, admiring the way the skintight skirt cupped her ample bottom. Why did the bad girls always look so good?

They stopped at the elevator and he pressed the down button. "How do you find out about these events? Is there some sort of website or something?"

"There are message boards and forums." With a ding, the elevator door slid open and she got in. "But I found out about this one from some friends. That's how I know it's okay."

He followed her inside and hit the button for the ground floor. "So my job's safe. I still don't understand how going to a rave is supposed to get Holcomb to endorse me."

"Your boss wants you to be more relaxed, more spontaneous, right?" She did a little shimmy, bringing her backside dangerously close to his groin. "There's nothing more freeing than dance."

Oh, yeah, that was freeing, all right. Any more freeing and he'd take her right there in the damned elevator.

He stabbed at the button again, as if that would speed their trip. This night was going be torture. In more ways than one.

Ding.

The elevator opened and Gabe hightailed it out of there. Maybe outside the cramped car he stood a chance of resisting her.

Right. And maybe he stood a chance of serving on the United States Supreme Court. She bent down to pull up one of her boots, simultaneously lifting her skirt and lowering her tube top, and he swore under his breath. Like she wasn't showing enough skin already.

"I'll get us a cab." Without so much as a backward glance, he strode across the lobby, through the door and to the curb, his arm raised. The sooner this evening started, the sooner it would end.

"Not so fast." Devin yanked his arm down and dragged him toward Canal Street. "Tonight we're slumming it."

She pointed down the block toward the subway station.

"You consider the subway slumming it?"

"No. But I figured you would."

"I take the subway. On occasion."

"Oh, yeah?" She paused at the top of the subway stairs and faced him. "When was the last time?"

He lowered his chin. "Okay, so it's been a while. But

only because I started biking to work when the weather got warm."

Her eyes traveled the length of his body and her tongue darted out to lick her lips. "It shows."

She brushed past him and headed down the stairs, giving him another view of her spectacular ass. He stood for a minute, his mouth open. Christ, she was bold. He'd never had a woman check him out so blatantly. He wasn't sure if he liked it.

Okay, that was a lie. He liked it. A lot.

"Are you coming or not?" Devin called from the bottom of the stairs.

Not yet. But maybe later...

He bounded down the steps, shaking off that thought as quickly as it had sprung up. Figuratively and literally. "Right behind you."

The subway ride was uneventful. If Devin singing with a street drummer and helping a guy dressed as Spiderman find his cell phone could be called uneventful. All in only three stops. When they got off, she led Gabe a few blocks to a large brick building.

"This is it?" He looked around. Quiet. Deserted.

"Just wait." She knocked on the heavy metal door.

"Dev!" The burly, bald-headed man who opened it greeted her with a bear hug. "Where you been, girl?"

"Here and there." She hugged him back. "Got room for two more?"

"For you, of course." He opened the door wider and eyed Gabe. "Who's your friend?"

"Carlos, this is Gabe. He's a virgin," she said with a wink.

"A what?" Gabe choked.

"She means it's your first rave." Carlos ushered them in and closed the door. "Don't worry. Devin's a real pro. She'll take care of you."

"That's what I'm afraid of," Gabe muttered.

Carlos showed them down a long hall and then a flight of stairs. As they descended, the insistent beat of techno music grew stronger, vibrating through the soles of Gabe's loafers and up his body.

He bent his head so his mouth was at Devin's ear. "This might be a good time to confess I'm not much of a dancer."

"Don't worry. I'll lead." She grabbed his hand. "Just stick close and follow me."

"Have fun, kids." The music was deafening now, and Carlos had to yell to be heard as he swung open the door at the bottom of the stairs.

Gabe nodded in acknowledgment, not even bothering to try to shout over the noise, and he and Devin stepped into what seemed like another dimension.

The big open space was wall-to-wall people of all ages, from college kids to baby boomers. Some were dressed in street clothes like him. Others wore all manner of costumes: tutus, hot pants, sequined bras, fluorescent wigs, outrageous hats and glasses. Gabe could have sworn one woman's dress was made entirely of duct tape.

A huge stage filled the far end of the room, showcasing a DJ behind a wall of electronic equipment. Giant screens displayed images from an elaborate laser light show.

"Come on," Devin said, drawing him into the crowd. "Let's dance." Or at least that's what he thought she said. They didn't teach lip-reading at Columbia. Or Officer Development School.

The crush of bodies on what Gabe supposed could be considered a dance floor pressed them together, chest to chest, hip to hip. Laughing, Devin threw her head back and raised her arms. Then she started moving, swaying, undulating against him and he thought his cock would burst through his khakis.

"What are you doing?" he mouthed.

She smiled and looped an arm around his neck, tugging him impossibly closer. He tensed, certain she could feel his erection straining against his zipper.

Christ. What had happened to his legendary self-control? The guys at work called him Mr. Spock, and it wasn't because he had pointy ears.

Gabe gritted his teeth and focused on a spot somewhere just above Devin's left shoulder. Anything to distract him from the seductive way her breasts shimmied under her tiny tube top.

With her free hand, she grabbed his waist. "Move those hips," she shouted. "You're as stiff as a freaking statue."

Oh, he was stiff all right. But not in the way she meant. "I told you, I can't dance."

She rose up on her toes to speak into his ear. "Just think of it as sex standing up. With your clothes on. In public." She gave him a wicked grin. "You can do that right?"

He smiled back. "I can try."

"Good."

She started swaying again, using the hand at his waist to make him move with her. After a minute, he relaxed and gave in to the rhythm of the music and the soft but insistent pressure of her hand. With each step, each brush of her chest against his, his pulse quickened and his breath grew more ragged.

Gabe dragged his gaze from Devin's and scanned the crowd. It was either that or go from the simulated sex she called dancing to getting down and dirty for real right there in the middle of the floor.

A few gyrating bodies away, a man in a leather vest and pants was doing his best impression of moonwalking. He turned, and his eyes locked on Gabe. A slow, sardonic smile spread across his face as he held out his thumb and index finger in the shape of a gun. He pointed it at Gabe, then shifted his aim to Devin before pulling the imaginary trigger.

Fuck. Gabe knew that ugly mug. Had seen it in court every day for three months, felt those eyes boring into the back of his head from the gallery when the jury announced its guilty verdict and the judge pronounced sentence—life in prison without parole.

"We've got to get out of here," he yelled, unwrapping Devin's arm from around his neck. "Now."

"What—"

"No time for questions." He pulled her farther into the fray, away from both the mock gunman. And, unfortunately, the door they'd come in. "Is there another exit?"

"This way," she hollered back, taking the lead and pushing through the crowd toward the stage. "Like Carlos said, I'll take care of you."

"What the hell was that all about?" Devin asked when they were finally outside the building and she didn't have to scream her lungs out to be heard. One minute she was sure Gabe had been about to let go, to give in to the music and the crazy, crazy lust swirling between them. The next, he'd bolted for the door, colder than a flat frog on the Cross Bronx Expressway.

"Not yet." His eyes flicked from left to right, settling on an alley alongside the warehouse. "Come on. We can hide down here for a few minutes. I want to make sure we're not being followed."

"Followed?" She struggled to keep up with him despite her long legs. "What is this, *CSI*?"

"No." He ducked into the alley, grabbing her arm and pulling her into the shadows with him. "This is real."

The tone of his voice made goose bumps rise on her arms.

"What happened back there?" she whispered.

"Nothing you need to worry about."

"Then why am I cowering in an alley at one in the morning?"

He put a hand against the brick wall and let out a long, slow breath. "Let's just say I ran into someone I'd rather not see."

She surveyed the overflowing dumpster, the abandoned refrigerator, the puddle of something a little too close to her left boot that didn't look or smell like water. Mr. Clean had to be desperate to drag her into this cesspool. "You must really hate this guy. What'd he do to you?"

"It's what I did to him." Gabe gave her a sidelong glance. "I put his younger brother in prison."

"Oh." She nodded. "I can see how that'd piss him off."

"The guy was guilty."

"I believe you. But I'm guessing big bro was harder to convince." She wrinkled her nose. "How long do we have to hide down here? It smells like a sewer. And I think there's something moving in that pile of newspapers."

"Just a few more minutes." He poked his head around the corner then pulled it back again. "Until I'm sure the coast is clear."

She flexed her tired toes in her boots and looked for someplace to sit down. Her choices were a plastic milk crate with a hole through the bottom, an overturned five-gallon bucket that looked like it hadn't been washed since Obama took office or the suspicious newspapers. She gave up and leaned against the wall next to Gabe. "Not exactly what I had planned for tonight. But at least it's out of your comfort zone."

"I think it's safe to say this entire evening's been out of my comfort zone."

She turned her head to study him and found his eyes on her. Something in his stare made her breath catch, and it was a second before she could form a coherent sentence. "I don't know. I thought you were doing pretty good in there. A few more minutes and you'd have been glow-sticking with the best of them."

Or I'd have been dry humping you in the middle of the dance floor.

She tried to tell herself what she felt for him was purely physical. Gabe was a certified hottie. She'd have to be six feet under not to want him. That must be why her knees were wobbly and her heart was practically pounding out of her chest. Well, that or their sprint to the alley.

The trouble was she suspected it was something more. She was starting, God forbid, to actually like the guy. When she'd shown up at his apartment, unannounced and dressed like a throwback from the sixties, she'd half expected him to slam the door in her face. Instead, he'd been a good sport, going along with her crazy plan and letting her drag him and his two left feet onto the dance floor. Hell, she'd even been having fun until he went all cloak and dagger on her.

"Glow-sticking?" He shifted closer to her and rested his forearm against the wall above her head. The stench of the alley faded, replaced by a mix of toothpaste, soap and his woodsy cologne.

"It's pretty self-explanatory." She swallowed hard to relieve the sudden dryness in her throat. "You…"

"Quiet." He held up a hand.

"What the…?"

He cut her off with a finger on her lips as the sound of footsteps and distant chatter grew louder.

"Damn it, we lost him." A male voice, tight and gruff.

"Are you sure it was him?" Another man, this one higher pitched.

"Sure, I'm sure. Do you think I'd forget the face of the scumbag who locked Frank up?"

"What's a district attorney doing at a rave?"

"How the fuck should I know? Maybe he's undercover."

The footsteps stopped and Devin could just make out two hulking shadows at the mouth of the alley. Their backs to her, they looked like linebackers, big and bulky and capable of inflicting serious bodily injury without breaking a sweat.

Shit. The night had gone from bad to worse to flat-out disastrous.

She held her breath and shifted nearer to Gabe, who slipped his hand from her mouth to her wrist and pulled her around the Dumpster.

The sharp rasp of a match strike echoed in the muggy August air. "How about that chick he was with? Sweet piece of ass."

Instinctively, Devin lunged toward the voices, but Gabe held her back, wrapping a protective arm around her waist and tugging her against his rock-solid torso. She pressed her lips together, her heart beating fast from the threat of being discovered—and from Gabe's hot, hard embrace.

"Put that damn thing out. We don't have time for a smoke break. They can't have gotten that far. Come on."

The men moved off, their steps and voices fading into the darkness.

"Christ, that was close." Devin let out the breath she'd been holding and shuddered, prompting Gabe to wrap his other arm around her and draw her closer. "Think it's safe to head out?"

"Too soon." His mouth was at her ear, his lips tickling the lobe as he spoke. "We need to give them a head start."

"Sounds like a plan." He was too tempting, too close, the inexplicable pull he had on her too strong to resist. She spun in his arms so that the fringe on her tube top swung wildly, brushing his chest. "Got any ideas how we can pass the time?"

"Oh, I've got ideas." He loosened his hold and tried to

step away from her, but she followed him, twining an arm around his neck to keep him from escaping.

"Let me guess. Charades? Would You Rather? Pin the Banana Peel on the Dumpster?" Her hand threaded through the short crisp hairs at the nape of his neck, and she guided him with one knee, backing him up against the exposed brick of the warehouse. "Or maybe something a little more...intimate?"

"You realize we're on a public street, right?" He looked both ways like he was casing the area for witnesses. "Anyone could come along and find us. Hell, someone almost did."

She laughed softly and tossed her hair, making sure to give him a whiff of her perfume. Chanel No. 5. Endorsed by Marilyn Monroe and guaranteed to drive a man wild. Was that what she'd been planning when she'd given in to a last-minute whim and dabbed it on before leaving her apartment? She shook off the question and trailed a finger down his arm. "That didn't stop you from making out with me on my doorstep."

"I wasn't...myself that night."

Her wayward finger traveled up his chest and undid one of the buttons on his polo. "And you are now?"

"I'm not sure anymore."

She eased a leg between his, rocking into him.

He moaned. "You make me crazy."

"Crazy can be good." She tilted her head to run her lips along his jawline. "Very, very good."

"Or very, very bad." His silky voice was almost a caress, so low she barely heard him.

"That's what I'm counting on."

With a groan, he turned his head and their mouths met in a frenzy of need. His hands came up to cup her face, his grip gentle yet firm enough to keep her lips exactly where he wanted them. Devin sighed and relaxed against him, needing the support since her legs felt like two strands of overcooked spaghetti. She may have been the one to start the fire, but Gabe's kiss left no doubt who was in control now. And while she wasn't normally into the whole dom/sub thing, it was different with Gabe. Giving in to him felt right. Safe. And at the same time scary as shit.

After what could have been one minute or twenty, he lowered his hands to her shoulders and the kiss softened, his mouth more patient than plundering. She reached up to undo the last button on his polo, needing to see more of him, feel more of him, when something in the air made her break off.

"What's that smell?" She gave a little sniff.

He ran a hand through his hair and frowned. "We're in an alley. Everything smells. You've got to be more specific than that."

"I'm glad one of us can crack jokes." The pile of newspapers rustled and Devin had the sudden suspicion that whatever was under there was black and white and the source of the scent that interrupted their kiss. "Think we can get out of here before this night gets any freaking worse?"

"Oh, I don't know." Gabe tilted her chin so she was forced to look at him. Instead of the annoyance she expected to see, his eyes sparked with mischief. "It's had its moments. I can't wait to see what you've got in store for me next."

"Next?" Was he serious?

"But not tonight." He let go of her chin and took her hand. Together, they left the dim alley and stepped into the streetlamp-flooded street. "We've had about as much fun as I can handle in one evening."

5

"WHAT'S THE MATTER with you, man?" Cade Hardesty flopped into the bleacher seat next to Gabe and nudged him with his elbow. Beer sloshed from his plastic cup onto Gabe's Top-Sider shoes. "Not a cloud in the sky, the Yanks are ahead by three and Sabathia just struck out the side. And you're sitting there looking like you lost your best friend."

Gabe dabbed at the stain on his left shoe with a napkin. "Maybe I'm rooting for the Sox."

"Fat chance," Cade said when the cheering died down from Teixeira's lead-off single. "Your mind's been somewhere else the whole game. Bad week at work?"

"You could say that." The Park Avenue case was turning out to be a huge headache. No physical evidence. No motive. Nothing even missing from the apartment. And the only witness who could put the defendant in the area at the time of the murders was waffling more than Brett Favre in the off-season. It'd be a miracle if Gabe got it past the grand jury.

He wasn't having any better luck with Victor. Gabe had managed to dig up the name of his old caseworker, but she wasn't returning his calls. Maybe Monday he'd track her down at her office. Better that than disappoint Devin.

Devin.

Two times he'd been alone with her, and both had ended

the same way. With him hot, hard and horny. He had to keep reminding himself that their arrangement was a business deal, nothing more. That they couldn't keep their hands off each other was just an added complication. And the last thing he needed in his life right now was complications. Not when he was so close to climbing the next rung of his career ladder.

"Wanna talk about it?" Cade drained his beer and waved to the pretty, ponytailed vendor making her way up the aisle.

"What are we, girls?" Gabe sneered. "What's next? We paint our nails and give each other makeovers?"

"Hardly." Cade winked at the vendor and gave her a twenty. She blushed and handed back his change and two beers, one of which he passed to Gabe. "Ten bucks says next round I get her number."

"No bet." Gabe shook his head. He wasn't an idiot. Women flocked to Cade. He had an easygoing charm Gabe had never been able to master. Plus, the guy looked like a California surfer: buff, blond and perpetually happy. The polar opposite of Gabe, who had once been called Heathcliff on the moors by a particularly astute lit major he'd dated.

"Just as well." Cade shrugged and swigged his beer. "I'd hate for your week to get even worse."

A buzzing in his back pocket stopped Gabe's snappy comeback. He stashed his beer under his seat, pulled out his cell phone and swiped a finger across the screen to unlock it.

One new message. From Devin.

He hesitated, almost afraid to read it. Did she want to schedule their next little adventure? Or call the whole thing off? And which answer was he hoping for?

"Devin?" Cade peered over his shoulder. "Why's Elvira, Mistress of the Dark texting you?"

Gabe winced at the nickname he and Cade had come up with for her back when Holly had first brought Devin home to Stockton. She'd reminded them of the horror hostess, with her wide eyes, full mouth and long inky black hair. She'd acted like her, too, all moody and mysterious.

But she wasn't, not really. Okay, she was sassy and sharp and sarcastic as hell. But she was also full of light and life and…

"Are you going to open it or stare at your phone all damn day?" Cade asked.

"Open it." Gabe tapped the screen, thankful that Cade had interrupted his thoughts before they crossed into the danger zone. The strains of "Take Me Out to the Ballgame" rang through the stadium and the crowd stood for the seventh inning stretch and sang along.

Gabe joined them—in the standing, not the singing—and read Devin's message to himself.

Phase two. Tomorrow. 7:00 p.m. My place.

"Phase two of what?" Cade stood shoulder-to-shoulder with him, his eyes locked on the screen.

"Stop doing that. It's an invasion of privacy." Gabe turned away from his friend and texted back.

Where are you taking me this time?

He only had to wait a few seconds for a reply.

It's a surprise. You'll like it, I promise. No dancing.

He grinned and tapped out another message.

That's reassuring. But how will I know what to wear? I don't want to be caught with my pants down, so to speak.

Her answer came quickly.

I've got it covered. Just get your butt to my place. And
don't be late.

With a chuckle, he stowed the phone back in his pocket
and sat.

"So are you going to tell me what the hell's going on
between you and Devin?" Cade crossed his arms and
leaned back in his seat.

"It's nothing. Really," Gabe added when Cade raised
an eyebrow.

"Fine. Don't tell me, your best friend since kindergar-
ten. The guy who took the fall for you when you broke
your mother's antique vase. Who helped you move to your
first apartment in the city, up five flights of stairs. In July.
With no air conditioning. Who—"

"Okay, okay." Gabe held up his hands in mock surrender. "I get the point."

He paused, debating how much to reveal and opting
to leave out his part of the bargain. He had a feeling not
many people knew about Devin's brother, and he didn't
want to be the one to open that can of beans. "She's helping me with a problem at work."

"On a Saturday night? At her place?" Cade rolled his
eyes and took another slug of beer. "And what, she's a
lawyer now? Last I heard she tended bar and tattooed
the masses."

"Yes, yes and no, she's not a lawyer." Gabe reached
under his seat for his beer. Expensive Scotch and fine
French wines be damned, some occasions called for a
plain, old American Budweiser. And a ballgame on a sweltering summer evening was one of them.

"Then how the hell is she helping you?"

Gabe stared down at the field. Teixeira had a huge lead

off first, daring the catcher to pick him off. "I'm running for DA. Filed the papers last week."

Cade clapped him on the back. "Holy crap, man. That's fantastic. You'd make a great district attorney. New York would be lucky to have you."

"Thanks." Aside from Holcomb—and Devin—he hadn't told anyone his plans, not even his family. Cade's support meant more to him than Holcomb's. Unfortunately, it wouldn't get him any votes. "But they won't have me if I don't get my boss's endorsement. He wants me to be more relatable. A man of the people. That's where Devin comes in."

"What's she going to do? Turn you into some sort of political puppet?"

"Not exactly. Just loosen me up a bit."

"You know, there are professionals who do that kind of stuff. Image consultants, I think they're called. The captain brought one in to help the department deal with the backlash from that moron Frazier's sexist tweets."

"Yeah, I thought about calling one of them. But then I met up with Devin, and she offered to help, so…" Whatever lame excuse he was about to give got mercifully swallowed up by the cheers of the crowd as Teixeira stole second.

"Have it your way." Cade shrugged and turned back to the game. "But don't say I didn't warn you. That girl is trouble."

Right, Gabe thought as he tried to pay attention to what was going on down on the field. *Now where I have heard that before?*

"HERE." DEVIN DRAGGED Gabe into her apartment and thrust a pile of clothes at him. Blue Converse low-tops, faded jeans and a gray Pogues T-shirt. "Put these on."

Gabe checked the tags. "How'd you know what sizes I wear?"

"Holly." Devin gave herself a mental gold star for resourcefulness.

Gabe blinked. "You called her in Istanbul?"

"It was a fashion emergency." Devin pushed him toward the open bathroom door. "Now get your butt in there and put them on. We've got places to go and people to see."

"Yes, ma'am." He shot her a smile that could have powered the entire northeast grid, stepped into the bathroom and closed the door behind him.

She sagged against the wall and tucked a lock of hair behind her ear. She needed this to work better than her last brilliant idea. Gabe would probably bail on their arrangement if she screwed up again. And without him, her chances of finding Victor were next to nil.

She'd been patient, not wanting to bug Gabe for information about her brother. But it had been over a week. A little push wouldn't hurt, would it?

"Any word on Victor?" She bit her lip and waited for his answer.

"Not yet." His voice carried through the closed door. "I found his caseworker, but she hasn't returned any of my calls. If I don't hear from her by Monday, I'll...damn."

"What's wrong?" She moved to the door.

"These jeans are a little tight."

She barely suppressed a guffaw. "That's how they're supposed to be."

"My underwear is bunching up."

"Then take them off." She licked her lips, imagining him gloriously naked under all that blue denim. "It'll be our little secret."

She hoped to hell the rustling behind the door meant he was following her instructions.

"Uh, what should I do with these things?" he asked a minute later. "And the rest of my clothes?"

Jackpot.

"Just throw them in the hamper in the closet. I'll wash them for you. Consider it your reward for being a good sport." Not to mention insurance she'd see him again. Were guys as attached to their boxers as women were to their thongs?

The bathroom door creaked open and Gabe strode out with all the confidence of a runway model.

"Do I pass muster?" He did a slow turn for her inspection.

Pass? He'd gone straight to the head of the mother-loving class.

She'd gawked at him in a suit. Ogled him in business casual. But in the quintessential male uniform of faded jeans and a simple T-shirt?

Yum diddly dum dum dum.

The jeans hugged his delectable ass and showcased muscular thighs. The soft cotton shirt cupped his pecs then fell loosely over his taut stomach and abs, ending at his waistband. She sucked in a breath. Clearly, the guy hit the gym regularly. No one got a physique like that sitting at a desk all day. Even if he did bike to work.

"That bad?" Gabe raised a questioning eyebrow.

"Uh, no. You look great."

Lame, lame, lame. Time to cut her losses and get him out in public where she'd have less of a chance to make a complete fool of herself.

She grabbed her purse from the couch. "Let's go."

He followed her to the door. "Are you planning on filling me in on your plan?"

"We're going to a pub crawl in the Village." He started to speak but she cut him off. "Before you say anything, it's not all about the party. I learned my lesson last time. This is a cultural event."

"How is schlepping from bar to bar getting progressively more wasted cultural?"

"It's a literary pub crawl. Actors take us on a tour of bars where some of New York's greatest authors hung out, drank and wrote. Edgar Allen Poe. Eugene O'Neill. Louisa May Alcott. And it's all for charity."

"Are you serious?"

"As a knuckle tattoo."

"Wow, Devin that sounds…"

Her heart skipped a beat or ten while she waited for his reaction.

"…perfect. What's the charity?"

She let out a long breath she hadn't even realized she'd been holding and reached for the doorknob. "Turn the Page. We train volunteers to go into schools and work with kids who are struggling with reading."

She swung the door open. Always well-mannered, Gabe held it for her as she walked through. "We?"

Oops. She hadn't meant to let that slip. As usual, her brain went on strike around Gabe.

She locked the door behind them.

"Yeah, I help them out sometimes." More than sometimes, but this wasn't the time for true confessions. This night was supposed to be about getting Operation Loosey Goosey back on track.

"Sometimes, huh?" Damn. Looked like Mr. State's Attorney was just starting his cross-examination. With a hand on her back, he escorted her down the stairs. "Why is it I get the feeling you're holding out on me?"

"How should I know? I'm an open book." They reached the foyer and she stopped, her arms spread wide in a look-at-me gesture. "What you see is what you get."

Tough. Uncomplicated. Alone.

"You can't fool me. You want everyone to think you're a tiger." He tapped a finger to her chest, right above her racing heart. "But deep down you're just a big ole pussy-cat."

"Am not." She pushed open the door to the street and headed outside, needing to put a little distance between them. Who the hell was he, acting like he knew her better than she knew herself? And damn him for being right.

"Sure." Gabe sprinted to catch up to her. "That's why you're helping me win over Holcomb."

"Payback," she tossed over her shoulder. "For helping me find Victor."

"And why you're reading to underprivileged kids."

"I like Harry Potter."

He snickered. "If you say so."

"I do." She stopped at the corner. "Here we are."

"Already?"

She motioned toward the blue-and-white sign overhead. "The White Horse Tavern. Watering hole to icons Norman Mailer, Hunter S. Thompson and Frank McCourt. And the start of our tour."

Gabe smiled and took her elbow, pulling her to the side as a group of what looked like college students spilled out of the bar. "What are you, one of the guides?"

"Right." She shrugged off his hand, annoyed at the tingles spreading up her arm. "Like anyone would follow me anywhere."

"I would." He held the door open—that gentleman thing again—and waved her inside. "I did. I followed you here."

He was so close she could practically feel his six-pack pressing against her back. Her stammered response was swallowed up in the chaos of the bar as they made their way toward a crowd gathered across the room. A woman at the center broke from the group when she spotted Devin.

"Chica! You made it." She gave Devin a quick hug.

"I said I would. And I never break a promise."

"Who's the *guaperas*?"

Devin coughed discretely. "Ariela, Gabe. Gabe, Ariela."

He held out his hand. Ariela took it, holding on a little too tight and a little too long for Devin's liking. Not that Devin had any say in it. She and Gabe were friends. Not even. Acquaintances, really.

Who wound up with their tongues in each other's mouths almost every time they saw each other.

"What's a *guaperas*?" he asked. "Should I be insulted?"

"I wish." Devin crossed her arms in front of her chest.

"Far from it." Ariela eyed him up and down, the glint in her baby browns telegraphing her appreciation. "It's nice to finally meet one of Devin's friends. She's one of our best volunteers. Every Tuesday, like clockwork."

Devin shot her friend a look that could have stripped paint. "Ariela's brother owns the tattoo parlor where I work. She's the one who got me involved with Turn the Page."

"Every Tuesday, huh?" Gabe's normally somber eyes flashed with playfulness.

"Thursdays, too, sometimes, when we need someone to fill in. Devin's a real lifesaver. I wish my other volunteers had half her dedication." Ariela checked the time on her smart phone. "Time to get this show on the road. I'd better go corral the tour guide. I'll catch up with you both later."

"Thursdays, too," Gabe teased as Ariela sauntered back to the group. "That's a lot of Harry Potter."

"It's hard to say no to Ariela. She's a force of nature."

A pair of fellow volunteers waved Devin over to the bar, and she elbowed her way through the crowd toward them.

"Is there anyone you don't know in this place?" Gabe trailed after her.

"I don't know her." Devin jerked her head toward a statuesque blonde entering the bar. Way overdressed, probably in designer duds from head to toe. Not a hair out of place. Definitely not someone who'd stoop to associate with a tattoo artist/bartender with an earful of piercings and a piss-poor attitude.

Gabe stiffened and put a hand on Devin's shoulder, stopping her. "I do." His voice was strained. "That's my ex."

6

FIRST FRANK'S IDIOT BROTHER. Now Kara.

"Bourbon. Neat." Gabe slid a twenty across the bar to the bartender.

In a city of over eight million people, why was it so damned hard to steer clear of the handful he didn't want to see?

"Pace yourself." Devin shouldered her way into the spot next to him at the rail, waving off her friends. "We've got a long night ahead of us."

"Make it a double." He nodded toward Devin. "And whatever the lady's having."

She ordered a Jack and soda and waited until the bartender returned with their drinks. "Bad breakup?"

He sipped his bourbon. The strong, smoky liquid slid down his throat like velvet, warming him from the inside out. "More embarrassing than anything else."

"How long ago?"

He eyed Kara across the room. She didn't seem bored now, surrounded by a pack of fawning admirers. Had she seen him? Did he care? "A few weeks."

"So that night in the park…"

"Yeah." He nursed his drink. "We'd just split up."

He didn't bother filling her in on the details of his botched proposal. There was only so much humiliation a guy could take.

"Damn." She rested an elbow on the bar and stared into her Jack and soda. Then she straightened and snapped her head toward him. He could almost see the lightbulb flash on above her. "Wait a minute. All that bullshit about you being boring…"

Fuck. The last thing he wanted was for Devin to feel sorry for him because his ex thought he was as exciting as watching grass grow. Bad enough she knew about Holcomb.

"Was that because of her?" Devin's eyes shot razor blades at Kara. "What did she say to you?"

Double fuck.

"Attention, everyone." Ariela stood in the center of the room and tapped a glass with a spoon, sparing Gabe from answering. With a relieved sigh, he shifted his attention to their host.

"On behalf of Turn the Page, I'd like to thank you all for coming this evening. I'm sure you're all ready to get this party started, so I won't talk long. But I wanted to give a shout-out to a very special donor who's with us tonight."

Gabe didn't have to be a fortune teller to figure out who Ariela was talking about. She held out her hand, and Kara joined her, flipping her hair over her shoulder and beaming at the crowd, basking in the glare of the public eye.

Why hadn't he noticed that about her before? Now that he thought about it, she had an almost compulsive need to be the center of attention. Restaurants. Theaters. Concerts. The world was her stage, and he'd been nothing more than a bit player in her drama.

Thank God she'd said no.

Out of the corner of his eye he caught Devin, smirking over the rim of her glass. He couldn't imagine her courting the spotlight. Hell, she'd barely wanted to admit she volunteered, and when she did let it slip she'd downplayed her involvement.

"Without Kara Humphries and her family's foundation, none of this would have been possible," Ariela continued, interrupting Gabe's thoughts before he could analyze the significance of the fact that he was mentally comparing Devin to the woman whom, only weeks before, he'd planned to spend the rest of his life with. "We're so happy to have them aboard as sponsors for the first time this year, and we hope they'll be with us for years to come"

Kara's smile widened and she gave the crowd her best beauty-queen wave. The crowd applauded politely, with the exception of Devin, who made a gagging noise then covered it by coughing into her hand.

Ariela motioned toward a bespectacled young man in a gray herringbone fedora at the other end of the bar. "You've heard enough from me, so I'll turn things over to Josh, our tour guide for the rest of the night. Drink up, and give generously."

"Kind of a prima donna, isn't she?" Devin drained her Jack and soda and plunked her empty glass onto the bar.

"Your friend?"

"No. Your ex." She took his arm and dragged him across the hardwood floor toward Josh. "Come on. Let's get closer. I want to hear this. Legend has it Dylan Thomas drank himself to death here, and his ghost still comes back for his favorite corner table."

The next couple of hours were a blur of new faces, small talk and literary tidbits courtesy of Josh. With Devin at his side as they traveled from bar to bar, Gabe felt more and more at ease as the night wore on. It could have been the booze. But he didn't think so. He'd known to pace himself even without Devin's warning.

No, something else was lowering his inhibitions, making him comfortable navigating a sea of strangers.

Someone else.

Devin.

She'd called Ariela a force of nature, but Devin was the dynamo. She seemed to have an endless supply of energy, bopping from bar stool to bar stool, introducing him to everyone, picking up the slack when the conversation lagged.

"Having fun yet?" Devin asked midway through their third stop on the tour, Kettle of Fish, a basement bar with a divey, bookish vibe frequented by beatniks like Bob Dylan and Jack Kerouac.

"Surprisingly, yes." He rested a foot on the bottom rung of his bar stool. "Although I don't think I'll remember the names of half these people in the morning. Hell, I don't remember them now."

"You're doing great, all things considered." She glared at Kara, a few feet down the bar rail, then looked back at him, her eyes warmer. "There's hope for you yet."

"Thanks." He owed her. Big time. And not just for helping him break the ice. He was pretty sure she was responsible for keeping Kara at bay, too. The few times he'd thought his ex was about to approach him, Devin had stopped her with an evil eye and a possessive hand on his arm or around his waist. A hand that felt a little too warm. A little too familiar. A little too comfortable.

Not that he needed protection. Watching Kara holding court all night had only proved that marrying her would have been a colossal mistake. But it was nice to be the protected instead of the protector for a change.

"Just a few more minutes here, and we'll move on to the fourth and final stop on our literary and epicurean journey," Josh announced. "The Minetta Tavern, favorite haunt of poet E. E. Cummings and home of the famous Black Label burger."

Gabe's stomach grumbled at the mention of food.

"I need to make a pit stop." Devin handed him her half-full glass. "Try not to get in too much trouble while I'm gone."

"I'll wait until you get back to start anything." He set the glass on the bar behind him.

She sauntered off, her perfect ass swaying hypnotically in her cutoff shorts as she weaved her way through the packed bar. He shifted in his seat and reminded himself—not for the first time—of all the reasons why acting on the obvious chemistry between them would be a screw-up of epic proportions. Sister's best friend. Holcomb's endorsement. The upcoming election.

"Gabe."

A breathy voice interrupted the laundry list of excuses running through his mind.

"Kara." He swiveled on the bar stool to face her. "You look well."

"And you look—" she studied him "—different."

He shrugged. "It was time for a change."

"I hope it's not because of anything I said." She fiddled with the clasp on her trendy bag.

"Nope." He picked up his drink, swirled, sipped and stared at her. He wasn't trying to be rude. It was just that after weeks of wondering how he'd react if he saw Kara again, he didn't have much to say to her.

He checked the clock behind the bar. Where was Devin? He'd never understood why women took so long in the bathroom. What the hell did they do in there, anyway?

"Seriously, Gabe. I'm worried about you." Kara pulled out the stool next to his and sat, putting a hand on his thigh. Her shiny red nails were a stark contrast to the faded denim of his jeans. "The clothes. That girl you're with. I wanted to talk to you earlier, but I was afraid she'd come at me with a switchblade."

Christ, had she always been so judgmental? Yet another flaw he'd overlooked.

"I'm a big boy." He picked up her hand and removed it from his leg, relieved that he felt nothing when she touched him. "I can take care of myself."

"I'm sure you can, but..."

"Hey, babe." Devin came up behind him and snaked an arm around his waist. Her hand came to rest on his hip, sending a bolt of white-hot desire to his groin. "Sorry I got held up. The line was ridiculous. Miss me?"

She reached up on tiptoe and gave him a down-and-dirty, take-no-prisoners kiss, with just enough tongue to make it borderline obscene in a public place. He barely had time to reciprocate before she broke it off, sliding down his body and giving him a look that said *Sit back and hold on tight. This is gonna be a wild ride.* "That's okay. You don't have to answer. Your hard-on speaks for itself."

Kara gasped, and Gabe almost laughed out loud at the shocked look on her face.

"Are you okay?" Devin took a half step toward the other woman. "I know CPR. And the Heimlich maneuver."

"I'm fine." Kara held up a hand to stop her. "Thanks."

"Good." Devin turned to Gabe and laid a palm on his chest. One finger traced the lettering on his T-shirt. "What do you say we skip the last stop on the tour and go back to my place? I've never been a big fan of E. E. Cummings anyway."

"I don't know," he teased, finally getting the idea and playing along with her. "That Black Label burger sounded awfully good."

"I promise I'll make it up to you." She pressed a kiss to the hollow between his neck and shoulder, making his pulse jump.

"Well, in that case..." He picked Devin's purse up off

the bar and handed it to her. "It's been nice catching up with you, Kara."

The polite lie tripped off his tongue. He gave Kara a dismissive nod and put his arm around Devin, shepherding her toward the door. Devin returned the favor by slipping her hand into his pocket and squeezing his ass. His cock twitched and his mind burned with a question only Devin could answer.

Was she serious about going back to her place? Or was it all an act for Kara's sake?

PLAYING WITH FIRE, that's what Devin was doing. But damn if she could stop herself.

Something had snapped when she'd come out of the bathroom and that designer debutante had put her claws on Gabe. Then she heard what that bi…witch had said about her. Devin might have gone after her with a switchblade. If she still carried one. But she hadn't since she was nineteen, when Leo had convinced her that she didn't need it anymore. That she'd found a home. That she was safe.

She didn't feel safe now. She was on edge. Ramped up. *Horny.*

What had started out as a lighthearted game had turned super serious when she'd felt Gabe's reaction to their impromptu kiss pressing against her thigh. Then she'd gone and practically propositioned him.

Idiot.

So what now? Was she for real when she'd offered to "make it up" to him? Was he for real when he'd accepted?

There was only one smart, safe thing to do. Pretend it never happened. And if smart and safe weren't normally parts of her vocabulary, well, she wasn't going to dissect the reasons for her change of course now.

"I can't imagine what you ever saw in her." She shrugged off his arm and pried her hand out of his pocket.

He was right. The jeans were tight. She sneaked a peek at his butt.

Delicious.

"Devin."

She kept walking. Faster. "I mean beyond the perky boobs, flat stomach and long legs."

"Devin."

"And I suppose there was her ass…"

"Stop."

The tone of his voice, gruff and demanding, made her obey.

"Look at me." He stepped in front of her, swept her hair off her face and tilted her chin up, forcing her to stare into the fathomless gray depths of his eyes. "We need to talk."

So not part of her game plan. She folded her arms across her chest. "What's to talk about?"

"What happened back there…"

"With your ex?" She was trembling like a tenderfoot getting her first tat, and her cheek burned where his thumb rested.

"No." The offending thumb brushed her lower lip. "With us."

"There…there is no us."

"Don't." The noise of the traffic swirled around them, her heart beating in time to the rhythmic *thump thump* of the cars passing over a steel road plate.

"Don't what?"

"Act like you're not feeling it, too. Like— Watch out!" He yanked her out of the way of a late-night cyclist and swore. "Are you okay?"

She nodded, her pulse pounding for two reasons now.

"This is ridiculous." He glanced at the night sky and scrubbed a hand across his face.

"That's what I've been trying to tell you."

"Not this." He gestured between them. "This." He

flung an arm out toward Christopher Street. "The fact that we're having this conversation in the heart of the goddamn Village."

"You're the one who wanted to talk."

"Yeah, well, maybe I was wrong. Maybe the time for talking is over." He did a hasty scan of the area then pulled her into a nearby doorway, trapping her there with his body. "Ask me again."

A hot flush spread up her face. "Ask you what?"

"What you asked in the bar." He rested his forehead against hers. "About going back to your place."

So he was serious. They were really doing this.

Hot damn.

"Do you want to go back to my place?" *Bad idea.* Her breath rasped in her throat. She was supposed to be putting out the fire smoldering between them, not dousing it with gasoline.

But what a lovely way to burn.

"Hell, yes," Gabe croaked. She reached up to touch his face, but he grabbed her wrist and stopped her midway, lowering her hand slowly but not releasing it. "Not here. Not like this. No more doorways or alleys. This time we do it right. Slow and easy. Even if it takes all night."

Oh, yeah. A fucking lovely burn.

He pulled her to the curb and whistled for a cab.

"We can walk. Or the subway's just up the block…"

He shushed her with a finger to her lips. "I know you're a big fan of public transportation. But I'm done sharing you tonight."

Could mere words make someone come? Because Devin was pretty sure she almost had.

She pulled herself together and ducked into the open door of the taxi, sliding across the bench seat until she was pressed against the far door. If Gabe could wait, so could she, but only if he didn't touch her.

He gave the cab driver her address and flashed Devin a good-boy-with-bad-intentions smile that had her practically coming again.

It was a damned good thing her apartment was only a five-minute ride away.

"You're awfully quiet way over there," Gabe said as the cab pulled away from the curb. "Having second thoughts?"

Second, third and fourth, but she wasn't going to let him know that. What the fuck was wrong with her? When she wanted a guy, she wanted him. And she usually had him. No hemming and hawing, full steam ahead.

So why was it different with Gabe? She wanted him. He wanted her. It should be as simple as that.

The cabby jammed on the brakes in front of Devin's apartment building, saving her from answering. "That'll be six bucks even."

Gabe handed over a ten and got out without waiting for change. He extended a hand to Devin, and she took it before she could chicken out. A tremor ran through her at the contact.

"You can still change your mind." He dropped her hand, almost like he realized how much his touch affected her and wanted to make sure she was acting with her head and not her hormones. "I hear it's a woman's prerogative."

"Maybe." She exhaled slowly, reclaimed his hand and led him up the stairs. "But not this woman. Not tonight."

7

DEVIN'S APARTMENT WAS just like her. Cluttered. Eclectic. Fascinating.

But Gabe barely had time to notice the collection of *Game of Thrones* bobbleheads on a shelf over the sink in the tiny galley kitchen, the pile of cooking magazines on the living room end table or the stack of paperback romances by the front door. He had one thing on his mind and one thing only.

Devin. In his arms. Preferably naked.

The snick of the lock echoed behind him.

"Do you want something to drink?" She moved past him into the living area, flicking on lights as she went. "I've got beer in the fridge and a bottle of merlot stashed somewhere. Or there's coffee or water if you want something nonalcoholic."

He stared at her as she fluttered around the apartment. Picking up a dirty dish. Straightening a picture frame.

She was nervous. Ballsy, badass Devin Padilla was nervous.

He sat on the couch and patted the cushion next to him. "Come here."

"Or I could cook something if you're hungry." She took a few steps toward the refrigerator. "I've got eggs, cheese and a pepper I should use before it goes bad. I could whip up an omelet."

"I'm not hungry. Or thirsty." He leaned back and patted the cushion again, one corner of his mouth curling into an amused smile. "Come. Here."

She crossed to him, the spiked heels of her knee-high black boots tapping the wood floor with each slow, deliberate step, and lowered herself next to him on the couch.

"Tell me about your tattoos." He took her wrist and flipped it over, tracing the letters inscribed there. "What's this one?"

She hesitated for a moment before answering, thrown off track by his abrupt change of subject. Just as he'd intended. "It says 'not afraid to walk this world alone.'"

"I can see that." He continued to stroke the soft skin of her wrist, her pulse jumping under his fingers. "But what does it mean?"

"Have you heard of the band My Chemical Romance?"

"Can't say that I have."

"I didn't think so." She gave him a bemused smile. "It's from one of their songs, 'Famous Last Words.'"

"Pretty grim lyrics."

She shrugged. "I don't know. I always saw them as words of strength. Determination to keep on going, no matter what."

"Interesting interpretation." He hooked a finger under the straps of her bra and tank top, inching them off her shoulder to reveal a swath of red, orange and yellow on the swell of her left breast. "How about this one? A bird?"

"A phoenix." He nudged the straps further down to see more of the tattoo. Her lips parted and her breath tickled his cheek. "Rising from the ashes of my misspent youth."

"And the spider behind your ear?" His hand trailed up her neck and into her hair, pushing it back. It ran through his fingers like silk, releasing the fresh almond scent of her shampoo.

She tipped her head back, encouraging him to explore

further. "That was my first tattoo. I was barely eighteen. And monumentally stupid. I thought it made me look tough."

"It makes you look dangerous." He bent his head and nipped, then licked the spot. She tasted like honey and marshmallows and warm, willing woman, and he wanted more. Way more. "Sexy. Are there any others I don't know about?"

With one finger, she traced a path up his inseam to his waistband and toyed with the button there. "Why don't you undress me and find out?"

Her voice was thick with desire. He looked around the room for a door or a hallway. Something, anything that led to her bedroom. He needed a little more maneuvering room for what he had planned. A slow and steady seduction the likes of which Ms. Walking-the-World-Alone had most likely never let herself experience. "Bed?"

"You're sitting on it. The couch folds out. It's actually pretty comfortable."

"Sweetheart, at this point it could be a rusty cot in Sing Sing and I wouldn't care." As long as he could lay her out and feast on her as if she was his private, personal Thanksgiving banquet.

"I'll bet you've got a California king."

"Not quite, but it's big enough. We'll have to try it out sometime." He rose, pulling her up with him. In a hot second, he had the cushions off and was reaching for the handle under the mattress. "But for tonight, this'll do just fine."

He said a silent prayer of thanks when the thing sprang open without much effort, already made.

She yanked the hem of her tank from under her cutoffs and started to lift it over her stomach, but he stopped her with a raised hand. "I believe you offered me that pleasure. Lie down. I want to uncover those tattoos one by one. Like the seven wonders of the world."

"So you're the Indiana Jones of body art now, huh?" She raised an eyebrow but complied, letting her shirt fall and positioning herself across the bed. Propping her head up on one hand, she gazed at him with a hint of devilment in her eyes. "I should probably warn you. There are more than seven."

He met her gaze. "I'm up for the challenge."

"What about you? Aren't you going to get naked?"

"Ladies first." He knelt and lifted one of her feet, the leather of her boot smooth and cool under his hot palm. "As much as I'd love to have your legs wrapped around me in these, they have to go."

"Something else for next time, I guess." She sighed as he pulled her boot off and his hands returned to caress her toes, her instep, her heel, the pale skin of her calf, a spot at the back of her knee that made her moan.

Next time.

Her words reverberated in his head as he repeated the process on her other leg. *Oh, yeah.* She might not be willing to admit it yet, but he was getting to her. Breaking through the brassy bravado she used to keep everyone at arm's length.

Not for long. The Devin the world saw was just her hard exterior, her protective armor. He'd gotten glimpses of what lay beneath when she talked about her brother, or Leo or teaching kids to read. And those glimpses only whetted his appetite. He wanted to unearth more than her tattoos.

But they'd do for a start.

"What do we have here?" He examined one ankle, then the other, his thumbs moving over the twin hearts etched on each one. "A matched set?"

"Not quite." She moistened her lips and parted her

legs slightly. "The left has my initial inside, the right has Victor's."

"Nice." His hands moved up her bare calves. "Nothing here?"

She shook her head. "You have to go a little…higher."

"Like here?" He snuck a hand under the frayed edge of her cutoffs.

"You're getting warmer."

"How about here?" The hand traveled up her thigh to her crotch, making her suck in a sharp breath.

"Warmer."

"Here?" He brushed her hipbone and she shivered.

"You're burning up."

"No, sweetheart." With his other hand, he unbuttoned her shorts. The lacy fabric of her do-me-red panties teased his knuckles as he lowered the zipper. He eased the cutoffs over her hips and down her long legs, leaving her flushed and panting, wearing only the naughty undies and skimpy tank top. "You are."

BURNING UP? THAT WAS putting it mildly. More like spontaneously combusting.

Was that possible?

"Please," Devin moaned, hating herself for begging even as the word escaped her lips. She was supposed to be running this show, not Mr. Nice Guy. How had she lost control so far, so fast?

Gabe lay next to her on the bed—still fully clothed, damn it—and she swung a leg over his hips, straddling him. It was time for her to get the upper hand before he teased her into oblivion.

"Not so fast." He rolled her onto her back and held her there with the weight of his long, lean body. "I'm not finished exploring. By my count I've got at least three more tattoos to discover."

She arched against him, begging with actions now instead of words. "They're not going anywhere. Can't you finish your inventory later? I need to come."

If she thought her crudeness would shock him, she was wrong. Gabe grinned down at her like she was a pitcher of ice-cold beer and he was dying of thirst. He dipped a finger into her panties, skimming the top of her pussy, temptingly close to her aching clit. "Oh, you're going to come all right. Multiple times."

"Now." She rolled her hips. The movement only made him withdraw his finger, frustrating her further.

"Trust me. It'll be worth the wait." He raised her shirt over her stomach, and she sat up part way, helping him yank it over her head and off, exposing a red lace bra that matched her undies. "Now about those tattoos…"

He mapped each one with his fingers, his lips, his tongue. The starfish on her hip. The wood nymph on her shoulder. The chain of daisies around her belly button. The sugar skull, a colorful symbol of Mexico's Day of the Dead, on her lower back.

Devin was about ready to climb the walls when he finally reached for the clasp of her bra.

"I think it's time we lose this, too." Gabe peeled it off with maddening slowness, like he was uncovering a priceless treasure. When he was done, he tilted his head and admired his handiwork, his eyes dark and heavy-lidded, before moving in for her panties. "And these."

They quickly went the way of her bra.

"Now you." Devin grabbed at the waistband of his jeans.

"I told you." He gave her a hard, fast kiss—the first of the night, she realized, bewildered—then slid down her body, putting his fly out of reach. "Ladies first."

"Gabe." She gasped as he kissed and licked his way past her breasts to her rib cage, her navel and beyond.

"Oh my God." She gasped again when his warm breath fanned over the strip of hair she'd left above her pussy.

"Damn. You're so sensitive." His hand joined his mouth, and he curved a finger inside her. "So wet."

She jerked in response, desperate for him to find the spot that would send her over the edge.

"What's the matter, sweetheart?" He added another finger, pumping them slowly but still missing that all-important pleasure point. "No one ever take his sweet time with you? Worship every inch of your heavenly body? Make sure you're satisfied before worrying about himself?"

"Not as much as I'd like." She writhed beneath him and clutched his shoulders, her fingernails digging into the skin through the thin fabric of his T-shirt.

"That's what I love about you. Your honesty. At least when it comes to sex. As for the other stuff…" His lips hovered over her mound. "We'll get there. Eventually."

She didn't have time to dwell on his use of the word "love." Or wonder what "other stuff" he was talking about. His tongue swept across her labia and he buried his face in her folds, sucking and lapping at her with the same single-minded intensity he approached everything in his life. She moaned and let one leg fall off the edge of the bed, opening herself to his sensual assault.

He tugged at her clit, drawing it into his mouth and sucking furiously, bringing her to the brink of release. But before she could get there, he lifted his head and gave her a told-you-so smile. "Still with me?"

"Yes, dammit." She fisted his hair, trying to push him back down. "Don't stop. I'm so close."

"See what I mean?" His smile widened. "Honesty. The kind that deserves a reward."

He dove back in and with one swipe of his tongue sent her pussy into spasms. She held her breath as her orgasm rolled through her like thunder before a summer storm. At its peak, she called out his name as if to remind herself that the guy she'd always thought of as a bit of a prude—a smoking hot prude, sure, but a prude nonetheless—had been the one to reduce her to a boneless, quivering mass of spent desire. And how.

"That was some reward," she said a few minutes later when coherent thought had somewhat returned.

"I'm glad you approve." He stood, shucking off his sneakers and shedding his T-shirt. The tight jeans were molded to his thighs and groin, showing off an already impressive erection. "But that was just the beginning. Are you ready for me?"

"I've been ready since the White Horse." She raised herself up on her knees, her eyes locked on the bulge in his jeans, and yanked on his waistband. "I want you inside me."

He bent down and kissed her, and she could taste herself on his lips. "Hold that thought."

He pulled his wallet from his back pocket.

"Jackpot." He dropped the wallet, a goofy grin on his face and a string of condoms dangling from his fingers.

She rested on her heels and smiled back at him. "Pretty cocky, aren't you?"

"More like cautiously optimistic." He pushed his jeans down over his hips and kicked them off. His erection jutted out proudly, long and thick, the tip glistening with moisture.

"Aye, mami."

His grin got goofier and wider. "Now that's what a guy likes to hear."

Typical male.

"You know what they say." She tossed her hair over her shoulder and gave him the once-over. Again. Her sex tingled with the knowledge that his monster of a cock would soon be filling her, but she couldn't resist teasing him. "It's not the size of the boat. It's the motion of the ocean."

"Then be prepared for a tsunami. Because I don't think I'm going to be able to hold back once I'm inside you." He climbed onto the bed and ripped off one of the condom packets, tossing the rest on the end table. He tore it open and rolled it on, the glint in his eyes telling her he liked the way she watched his hands slide over the head of his penis and down the shaft.

"I don't want you to hold back. I want all of you."

"You won't be saying that if I come in sixty seconds."

She sat up and took his face in her hands, loving the scrape of his five-o'clock shadow against her palms. "That just means we can do it all over again sooner."

He quirked a brow at her. "That's an interesting way of looking at it."

"What can I say? I'm a glass-half-full kind of gal."

She drew him in for a lengthy, heated kiss. Lips clashed, tongues tangled, hands wandered. After a few minutes, he softened the kiss and lowered them both onto the mattress.

Damn the man. How was she supposed to keep her emotions in check, remember that this was just physical, a chemical reaction between two consenting adults, when he went and got all tender and considerate on her?

She wasn't. She couldn't.

"Gabe," she panted when he finally broke the kiss. "Don't stop."

"Stopping is the furthest thing from my mind right now."

He moved over her and she parted her legs to accommodate him. He teased her pussy with the head of his cock before slowly, maddeningly easing his way into her warm, wet center.

"Yes," she whispered, winding her legs around him and arching her back, pulling him deeper inside her.

He loomed over her, the muscles of his arms and chest rippling, his normally slate gray eyes darkened to a deep charcoal. "God, Devin. You feel so good."

"So do you." She brought her mouth to his chest, swirling her tongue around his nipple. "Taste good, too."

He moaned.

"You like that?" She nipped his ear. "How about this?"

He answered by thrusting harder, faster.

"Gabe, I'm going to come." She tightened her legs around his hips and grabbed onto his biceps, afraid she might float away on a cloud of sexual bliss if she didn't anchor herself to something. Someone.

"Do it." He touched his forehead to hers, those charcoal eyes boring into her as though he could see straight through her, into that secret part even she didn't fully understand. "Let go for me."

"Only if you come with me."

"Right behind you, sweetheart."

One, two, three more thrusts and she shattered, the tension that had been building in her bursting like water through a damn, flooding her body with wave after wave of pleasure. Gabe rocked against her and shuddered as he followed her over the edge.

They lay there like that, joined, sweat-drenched and spent, until he rolled her onto her side and withdrew, leaving her only long enough to dispose of the condom. She sat up and scooted to the edge of the bed.

"You okay?" He sat beside her.

"Couldn't be better." She picked up the packets he'd deposited on the end table and inspected them. Only two left. Damn. "Except for one thing."

He frowned. "What's that?"

She pushed him down on the bed and straddled him.

Sure, it had been fun—okay, mind-blowing—letting him take over. But now it was her turn to be in charge, and she was going to drive him as crazy as he'd driven her. And enjoy every minute of it.

She put the packets within easy reach on the bed and crawled down the length of him until her mouth was poised at the tip of his already stiffening cock. "We're going to need more condoms."

8

THE SMELL OF fresh-brewed coffee woke Gabe the next morning. He rolled over and reached for Devin, momentarily disappointed to find her gone until he heard the sound of running water coming from the bathroom.

Shower sex. Perfect way to start the day.

Especially if it was anything like the fold-out-couch sex they'd had last night. And the kitchen-counter sex. And the against-the-wall sex.

And still it wasn't enough.

Gabe jumped out of bed, sprinted to the bathroom and jiggled the door handle.

Locked.

"Hey, babe, let me in. I can scrub your back." He ran a hand across his jaw. Christ, he needed a shave. Then again, maybe Devin liked the rugged, bad-boy look. "Or your front, if you prefer."

He pressed his ear to the door.

Nothing.

He shrugged, figuring she must not be able to hear him over the running water, and went back to the living/bedroom. He found his jeans on the floor and snatched them up, feeling suddenly self-conscious strolling around her apartment in the buff. As he pulled them on, the shower shut off and he heard the scrape of the curtain being drawn back.

He pictured her stepping out of the tub, gloriously nude, water dripping off her firm, full breasts. Shower sex might be out, but après-shower sex could be just as good.

Gabe sat on the bed, willing his hard-on to behave until Devin emerged from the bathroom. To distract himself, he studied her apartment in the light of day. She had a hell of a lot of artwork. Reproductions, for sure, on her budget. But nice ones. Everything from a framed Degas print he recognized because his sister Noelle, a ballet dancer, had the same one hanging over her mantle to a miniature of one of Louise Bourgeois's spider sculptures.

He wandered over to a stack of what looked like canvases facing one wall. He flipped the first one around and took a step back.

Damn.

This was no reproduction. And he was no art critic, but it was stunning. Compelling.

Erotic.

The paint practically leaped off the canvas, drawing the viewer's eye to the image of a man and woman in what might have been a traditional picnic scene except for one thing. They were both naked. The woman reclined on a blanket in the foreground, her head back, eyes closed. Her breasts were thrust out proudly and one knee was bent, the artist only hinting at the shadowy area between her thighs. The man sat behind her, one hand on her raised leg, his lips at her nape. All around them lay the remnants of their feast—squashed sandwiches, spilled wine glasses, an overturned bowl of strawberries—leaving no doubt as to what they'd been up to.

"What the fuck are you doing?"

Gabe turned to face Devin, still beautiful in just a towel tied over her breasts, her wet hair streaming down her back, her hands on her hips and steam practically coming out of her ears. And not from the shower. "I didn't hear you come in."

"Obviously. Do you always snoop through your lovers' personal belongings the minute their backs are turned? What do you want to search next? My medicine cabinet? Maybe scroll through the messages on my cell phone?"

Personal? Did that mean...

"Did you paint this? It's amazing." He pointed to the rest of the canvasses. "What about these?"

The hands on her hips balled into fists. "I think it's time for you to go."

"Look, I'm sorry. I didn't mean to pry. But you have to know you're good. You should be exhibiting this stuff in a gallery, not hiding it in your apartment." He rubbed a hand through his hair. "You know, my sister Ivy has a friend who works at a gallery in Chelsea. Maybe she could..."

"No. No friend. No gallery." She hitched up her towel, which had started to slip, depriving him of a glimpse of the breasts he'd fantasized about when she was in the shower. The ones he'd nipped, licked and sucked last night until she'd screamed his name and come apart in his arms.

He shook his head, willing himself to focus on her artwork, and not what was under the scrap of terry cloth she was clinging to like a life preserver. "But..."

"And no buts." She bent to pick up his T-shirt and held it out to him. "You need to get dressed and get out of here. I'm due at work in an hour."

"On a Sunday?"

"We're open seven days a week at Ink the Heights." She tossed the shirt at him.

He caught it against his chest. "I don't understand why you waste your time with tattoos when you could be a serious artist."

Shit.

If he hadn't known the minute the words left his mouth

that they were a mistake, the pissed off look on her face sure as hell told him so. She was definitely steaming now, her expression saying, "Die, moron."

"I don't give a fuck whether you understand or not. It's my life. My choices. And as far as I'm concerned, I am a serious artist, and I'm not wasting a damn thing." She picked up a sneaker and threw it at him, smirking when he struggled to catch it with the T-shirt still in his hands. "Now like I said, get dressed and get going."

"Fine. I'll go." He pulled the shirt on over his head. If there was one thing he'd learned in the military-strategy class he'd taken as part of his Navy JAG training it was that pushing full speed ahead wasn't always the best option. Sometimes you needed to retreat and regroup before moving forward. "But this isn't the end of our discussion."

He didn't give her a chance to disagree, striding over to her and silencing her with a swift, searing kiss. "I'll call you when I have news about Victor. And I'll be waiting to hear what our next adventure's going to be."

She crossed her arms in front of her chest, whether to better hold up the towel or because she was still royally ticked at him he wasn't sure. "Haven't we had enough adventures already? You seemed pretty comfortable with all those strangers on the pub crawl. I think you're ready for the campaign trail."

"No way." He dropped the shoe and put his hands on her shoulders, loving the way her skin felt, soft and damp from the shower. "The only reason I was able to put three words together was because you were there with me every step of the way. You can't abandon me now."

"I'm not abandoning you. More like pushing you out of the nest." Her eyes softened, some of their anger gone. "You're ready to fly, Gabe. You just needed someone to show you how."

"What if I can't fly without you?" He massaged her shoulders. "What if I don't want to?"

She shook her head. "Don't say things you don't mean."

"I never do."

"You're an attorney. Isn't stretching the truth part of your job description?"

"I'm an officer of the court, sworn to uphold truth and justice."

A half smile played around the corners of her lips. "So you really are Dudley Do-Right?"

"In a manner of speaking." He gave her another quick kiss, softer this time. Then he picked up the sneaker and scanned the room for its mate, retrieving it from under the still unfolded couch. "Now, if I'm not mistaken, you've got bodies to tattoo. And I've got cases to close." And her brother to find.

"On a Sunday?" she asked, her tone mocking his earlier comment.

"I'd rather spend it in bed with you, but since that's not an option…" He sat, putting on the sneakers. "Until next time."

She moved to a closet in the corner, opened it and started rummaging around, pulling out pieces and tossing them on the bed. Denim skirt. Black tank top with the Ink the Heights logo on it. A couple of scraps of lace that had him adjusting his jeans. "Who says there's going to be a next time?"

"I do." Gabe stood. "And so do you."

She turned to face him, a high-heeled shoe in one hand. "How do you figure that?"

"Your nipples. They're practically poking holes through that poor towel."

He just managed to duck the shoe and close the door on his way out.

"HEARD YOU WERE in over the weekend." Jack strolled into Gabe's office Monday morning as if he owned the place—as usual—and threw himself into one of the guest chairs. Christ, the guy was a drama queen. "Hoping a little brown-nosing will get you that endorsement?"

Gabe closed the file he'd been reading. "I'm busy, Jack. So unless you have some reason for this visit other than to harass me about the election…"

"Actually, I have two." He dropped a thick folder onto Gabe's desk.

"What's this?"

"A copy of my nomination papers. I'm running against you." With a grin, Jack leaned back in his chair and propped his feet up on Gabe's desk. "Filed as soon as the clerk's office opened. Thought I'd let you know before the media got wind of it."

Shit. Gabe's stomach plummeted fifty stories. The guy might be a halfway decent lawyer, but the last thing Manhattan needed was an opportunistic bastard like Jack as district attorney. He'd turn the whole office into a nepotistic nightmare.

"How considerate." Gabe picked up the folder and tossed it into the garbage. "Now get your goddamn feet off my desk and get the hell out of my office."

"Don't you want to know the other reason I'm here?"

"Not particularly."

Jack crossed an ankle over one knee and made a show of brushing off his oxford. "Holcomb wants to meet me at noon. You know what that means. You can kiss your precious endorsement goodbye."

"Could be." Gabe tried his hardest to sound unconcerned. He wouldn't put it past Holcomb to conveniently forget their San Gennaro deal and throw his weight behind Jack. "Or could be any one of a million things he wants to discuss with you. What makes you think it has anything to do with the endorsement?"

"A little birdie told me."

"The same little birdie who told you I was working yesterday?"

"Maybe, maybe not." Jack smoothed back his already slick hair. "A good investigator never reveals his sources."

"He took you off the Park Avenue homicide." Gabe twirled a pen between his fingers. "That doesn't sound like a ringing testimonial."

"Please. That case is a dead dog loser. Not what the future district attorney needs on his track record." Jack stood and crossed to the door, stopping and turning just inside the frame with a self-satisfied smirk. "Face it, pal. Holcomb's throwing you to the wolves."

Jack made his escape before Gabe could strike back. Not that he had much to say. Bottom line: Jack was right. The Park Avenue case was shit. Gabe had barely gotten an indictment from the grand jury. He'd never get a conviction without more than a shaky eyewitness.

Gabe swore under his breath, threw the pen down and reached for the phone to call the inspector he'd sent to canvass the neighborhood. Again. He had his hand on the receiver when it rang.

"Gabe Nelson."

"Attorney Nelson, this is Genevieve Brewer at Child Protective Services. You're looking for information on Victor Padilla?"

Finally. Maybe his day was turning around.

"That's right."

"I pulled his file. The good news is he was adopted in 2001, but I'm afraid that's all I can tell you. His adoption records are sealed."

Or not.

"I thought that might be the case." He took off his

glasses and rubbed the bridge of his nose. "Can you give me his last known address before the adoption?"

She rattled off an address in Brooklyn. "I'm sorry. I wish I could give you more information. But without a court order, there's really nothing I can do."

"I understand." He slumped in his seat. "No apology necessary. Thanks for getting back to me."

He hung up the phone and swore again.

Another dead end. Devin had hit roadblock after roadblock searching for Victor, and he had to tell her she'd hit one more.

Unless…

Gabe picked up the phone and dialed his inspector. A former cop, Dallas Murphy had been Gabe's righthand man from his first day as an assistant district attorney—following leads, interviewing witnesses. If anyone could find Victor, he could.

Murphy answered on the second ring. "Hey, boss. Nothing yet here. But you know how we thought the surveillance camera in the lobby was on the fritz?"

"Yeah."

"Turns out it was working just fine. And the security company's got the tapes from the day of the murder."

Halle-freaking-lujah.

"Great. Work up a warrant. I'll get it in front of a judge ASAP."

"You got it. Anything else?"

"Yeah." Gabe rose, crossed to the door and closed it. "But this is off the books, on your own time. Keep track of your hours and bill me."

"Now you've got my attention."

"Good. Got a pen and paper?"

"Ready, boss. Shoot."

Gabe was brimming with renewed determination when he ended the call a few minutes later. He might not have any answers for Devin beyond the fact that her brother had been adopted. But he wasn't done trying. Not by a long shot.

And he wasn't done trying with her, either.

He pulled his smartphone out of his pocket. What was the name of that bar she worked in? He'd been there once with Holly but that had been ages ago. All he remembered was that it started with an *N* and was around the corner from their apartment building.

A few taps and he had the information he needed. He'd given her a couple of days to regroup. Now it was time for him to make the next move.

It was past eight when Gabe pushed open the door to Naboombu. He'd called ahead to make sure Devin was working, hanging up the phone like a ten-year-old when she answered. Not because he was afraid to talk to her but because he wanted to surprise her, catch her off guard and throw her off her game.

Another tactic he'd learned from the JAG corps. With Devin, he wasn't above taking any advantage he could get. God knows, he needed every last one.

The bar was pretty crowded for a weeknight. Not hopping by any means, but a fair number of people occupied the oak stools, most watching the Yankee game playing on the flat-screen TV.

Gabe slid onto a vacant stool and looked for Devin. He spotted her at the other end of the bar with five shot glasses lined up in front of her and a stack of shakers, one inside the other, in her hand.

His eyes—and the eyes of every other guy in the place, even the ones who'd been focused on the ball game— zeroed in on her as she made an impressive display of tipping the stack of shakers and filling the glasses simultaneously. When she finished, she handed out the shots, flipped her long curtain of dark hair over her shoulder and bowed.

Applause broke out at the end of the bar.

"Encore."

"Yeah, do it again."

"Can you dance on the bar like the chicks in that *Ugly Coyote* movie?" a man with a horseshoe mustache asked.

Devin tossed the shakers into the sink behind her and grabbed a rag. "It's *Coyote Ugly*, genius. And I'm not Tyra freaking Banks."

"You can say that again." Mustache man knocked back his shot.

She wiped down the surface of the bar, slung the towel over her shoulder and headed toward Gabe's end of the bar. When her eyes caught his, they narrowed and her steps slowed.

"What are you doing here?"

He gave a halfhearted shrug. "Same as everyone else. Watching the game. Having a drink, if the bartender ever serves me."

"But why here?" She stopped in front of him, hands on her hips. "There's plenty of bars in Tribeca."

"Would you believe me if I said I like the ambiance?" A smile crept across his face.

She stared him down. "Hell, no."

His smile faded as quickly as it had appeared. "How about if I said I had some news about Victor?"

The air between them seemed to thicken. Gabe sucked in a breath and waited for her answer. Had he made a mistake bringing up her brother? He didn't have much information for her. And he didn't want to get her hopes up by telling her about Murphy. But maybe just knowing Victor had been adopted instead of languishing in foster care would relieve some of her concern.

After a long moment, she plunked an empty shot glass upside down on the bar in front of him.

"Then I'd say you can have whatever you want." She leaned an elbow against the bar and tucked her hair behind her ear. The smell of her almond shampoo wafted toward him. "On the house."

9

Devin's hand shook as she poured Gabe the Scotch and soda he'd ordered.

"So." She slid the glass across the bar to him. "You've found Victor?"

"Not exactly."

Her spirits did a nose dive. Her disappointment must have shown on her face because Gabe reached around the glass to take her hand.

"But it's a step in the right direction." He gave her hand a reassuring squeeze. "Your brother was adopted."

"Adopted?" She sagged against the bar. "When? By who?"

"The when I can answer. 2001." He sipped his Scotch. "But the who…"

She pulled back her hand. "Let me guess. The records are sealed."

He nodded. "I'm sorry. I know it's not what you wanted to hear."

"Thanks for trying." She took the towel from her shoulder and scrubbed at an imaginary spot on the gleaming oak bar, mentally calculating how long it would take to scrape together enough money to hire another private investigator. One who wasn't a lowlife, scum-sucking crook. Maybe Gabe could recommend someone.

He threw back the rest of his drink and set the glass

down with a resigned thud. "I wish I had something more. I know how important finding your brother is to you."

No. He didn't. No one did, really. Finding Victor wasn't just some silly quest so she could fulfill an idiotic childhood fantasy that they'd be reunited and live happily ever after. It was a matter of life and death. Or at least of Victor's safety and wellbeing. Victor was…different. Special. Finding out that he'd been adopted gave her a glimmer of hope, but what if his new parents weren't in the picture anymore? What if he was alone, in some piece-of-shit institution like the one in the newspaper article? Or, even worse, on the street?

Devin pressed her lips into a thin line, not wanting to think about the possibilities, each one more horrific than the next. She stopped scrubbing long enough to meet Gabe's eyes. "So I guess this is goodbye."

He caught her arm when she would have spun away. "Why do you say that?"

"Our bargain. You did what you could to find Victor. I got you ready for the campaign trail. What else is there?"

Except screwing like rabbits on Viagra.

His eyes darkened and his grip on her arm turned from possessive to playful, his thumb drawing figure eights on the sensitive skin at the inside of her wrist. "Do you really want me to answer that here?"

She scanned the guys at the bar. Except for the one who was slumped over with his head on his chest—she made a mental note to call him a cab—everyone was glued to the game on the flat-screen. "Why not? No one in here gives a shit about us. Besides, these guys have heard it all before. And then some."

Gabe continued to stroke patterns on her wrist, sending pinpricks of awareness up her arm and into her chest. "Don't say I didn't warn you."

"I'm a big girl. I can take it." She tried to pull her hand away but he held fast.

"Are you sure?" He tugged her closer, so close his breath stirred the hair behind her ear. "Because I'm not done with you, sweetheart. Not even close."

Promises, promises.

Devin shrugged off his words and took a step back, doing her best to feign indifference. "I told you, you don't need my help anymore. You're good to go for the election."

"You're wrong, but that's only part of what I need from you." He crooked a finger and she leaned back in to him, almost as if he was reeling her in on an invisible string, and rested an elbow on the bar. "A small part."

"What's the rest?"

"The rest?" He closed the remaining distance between them, his lips brushing against her earlobe as he spoke. "The rest is you naked. Those long legs wrapped around my waist. Your nails digging into my back. You screaming my name when you come. Think you can do that for me, sweetheart?"

"If she can't, sugar, I sure as hell can."

"Hey, Rue." Devin took a step back, breaking free from Gabe and the strange hold he had on her. She picked up the towel, which had dropped, forgotten, to the floor during their verbal sexfest, and reached for the vodka to make Ruby her usual gimlet. She was half pissed off, half grateful for the interruption. Her hand shook even more than when she'd made Gabe's Scotch and soda.

Damn him and his dirty talk. Talk that made her knees weak and her panties moist. Talk that wasn't supposed to come from straight-arrow district attorneys. Where had he learned to do that, speak so naughtily yet so beautifully?

Strike that. She didn't want to know.

Devin put the bottle back on the shelf behind her, wiped

her sweaty palm on her skirt and grabbed the lime juice from the minifridge under the bar. "Off early tonight?"

"Business is slow." Ruby hitched up her already short skirt and took a seat on the stool next to Gabe, batting her overly made-up eyes at him. "Unless Mr. GQ here wants to take me up on my offer."

"Bad idea." Devin stirred the drink with a neon orange swizzle stick. "He works for the DA."

"Shit." Ruby started to get up.

"No worries." Gabe waved her back down. "I'm not in vice."

"I'm almost sorry. I wouldn't mind having you hand-cuff me."

Ruby gave him her best eye-fuck, a move Devin had seen more times than she could count despite her repeated warnings not to do business in the bar. One of these days the owner was going to catch Ruby midtransaction and toss her spandex-clad ass out the door. Her profession aside, Devin liked Ruby. Hell, if it wasn't for Leo, Devin could've been working the streets alongside her.

"Plus, he's a prosecutor. Not a cop." Devin plunked the glass down in front of Ruby. "They don't arrest people."

"Pity," Ruby purred, her voice dripping sex appeal.

"I need a goddamn refill." A voice, thick and slurred with alcohol, rose from the end of the bar. "What's a guy gotta do to get some service around here?"

Crap. Sleeping Beauty had woken up. Thirsty.

"I'll take care of him." Gabe pushed back his stool.

"Sit down, Dudley Do-Right." Devin took the cordless phone from the receiver next to the cash register. "I got this. Dealing with asshole drunks is a job requirement. Unfortunately."

"What if I like riding to my woman's rescue?"

"First, I'm not your woman. And second, I don't need

to be rescued. Remember Central Park? I took care of Freddie, didn't I?"

"Have it your way." Gabe settled back in at the bar. "But when you're through dealing with our inebriated friend, you might as well pour me another Scotch and soda. I'm staying until your shift's over."

"The bar closes at two. And I've got to clean and lock up."

"No problem. I'll walk you home." Gabe nodded toward his new BFF, sitting beside him holding a compact mirror in one hand and attempting to apply devil-red lipstick. "Give Ruby one of whatever she's having, too. On me."

"Thanks." Ruby snapped the compact shut, tossed it and the lipstick into her handbag and toasted him with what was left of her gimlet. "You're all right for a government shyster."

"You're both nuts," Devin muttered as she dialed the cab company. "I don't know why I put up with you."

"Sure you do, sugar." Ruby's lips parted in a warped semi-smile. "You put up with me because I'm entertaining. And you put up with him because he's drop dead gorgeous."

"You didn't have to stick around." Devin punched in the code for the alarm on the keypad by the door, pulled it shut and tested the knob to make sure it was locked. "It's only a few blocks. I'm perfectly capable of getting myself home."

Gabe ushered her up the steps to the sidewalk, a hand at the small of her back. "Why do I feel like we've had this conversation before?"

"Why do I feel like we're going to have it again?" She hitched her purse onto her shoulder.

"Probably because we will." He dropped his arm, leav-

ing her back suddenly cool, even in the steamy August
heat. "We're both pretty stubborn."

"Speak for yourself." She gave him a subtle hip check,
telling herself the move was a sign of playful aggression
and not a desperate ploy to reestablish bodily contact.
"I'm nothing if not flexible."

"If you're talking physically, I can vouch for that." His
words conjured images of their Kama Sutra–inspired sex
session.

"I wasn't, but thanks for the seal of approval."

He laughed and reached for her hand. She hesitated
a second before taking it. Hand-holding wasn't part of
the protocol with the guys she typically dated. Too intimate. Too personal. But, then again, Gabe was about
as far removed from those guys as *Homo sapiens* were
from single-cell amoeba. It was like dealing with an entirely different species, one that wasn't scared off by a
little PDA.

His hand engulfed hers, soft but strong, and their fingers instinctively laced together with a familiarity that
usually came from years of experience. Devin took a deep
breath and exhaled in a slow hiss, the Sturm und Drang
of the city that never slept fading away.

Steady. The word thrummed through her like a dance
beat as they walked the rest of the short distance to her
apartment, a comfortable silence stretching between them.
Not boring. Not predictable. Steady. Gabe's boss and his
ex were idiots if they couldn't tell the difference.

"Well." With a pang of regret, she relinquished his hand
to dig her keys out of her bag. "Here we are."

"Yes." He leaned against the doorjamb and stuffed his
hands into his pockets. "Here we are. Again."

He followed her through the foyer and up four flights of
stairs to her apartment. She swung open the door, flipped
on the light and was halfway to her pathetic excuse for

a kitchen before she registered the absence of footsteps behind her. She deposited her purse on the counter and spun, hands on hips, to face him. "What gives? Aren't you coming in?"

He shook his head, not moving from the threshold. "Not tonight."

"It's going to be hard for me to wrap my legs around you if you're way over there." Using the counter for balance, she took off first one boot, then the other, wiggling her tired toes. "Unless that was all talk back at the bar."

"Hell, no." He gave her a wicked grin that made her privates tingle. "I fully intend to fuck you until neither one of us can stand."

"What are you waiting for?" She took a few steps toward him, releasing her hair from its ponytail and shaking it out.

"Friday."

"That's four fucking days away." Or fuck-less days. What red-blooded male waited that long to dip his wick into a wet and willing female? "So much for wanting me naked and screaming your name."

"Does this feel like I don't want you?" In three strides, he was in front of her, dragging her against his straining erection. "I want you today, tomorrow and the next day."

"Then what's the problem?"

"The problem is I want more than sex. I want a relationship. Coffee together in the morning. Watching Netflix on my sectional at night. All the everyday, getting-to-know-you stuff couples do. And I'm willing to wait until you do, too."

Devin shuddered and pulled away, backing up against the counter. "What if I said that I don't…can't…do relationships?"

"I'd say that's bullshit. I've seen you in action. You can do anything you set your mind to, if you want it bad enough." He moved in, trapping her between his hot, hard body and the cold, hard counter. "Do you?"

"Do I what?" She tilted her chin, trying to look more stubborn than sexed up, but the quiver in her voice gave her away.

He lifted a lock of her hair with one finger and let it fall. "Want it bad enough?"

"I...I don't know."

"Until you do, we'll have to settle for this." He braced a hand against the counter on either side of her and dipped his head for a kiss, fast and furious.

When he let her up for air, she had to cling to his biceps, bunching and shifting under the lush designer fabric of his suit jacket. He bent and spoke in her ear, soft and sweet and low. "Because when I take you again, it's going to be all of you, not just your body."

He gave her another quick and dirty kiss then released her and headed for the door.

"It'll never work." She collapsed against the counter, grabbing the edge in a white-knuckle grip to stop herself from crumpling into a hot-and-bothered heap. "We're light-years apart. Like the Bloods and the Crips. Or the Montagues and the Capulets."

"I'm going to prove you wrong, fair Juliet." He stopped at the door and turned, one hand on the knob. "Starting Friday."

Her mouth twisted in a scowl. "What's so special about Friday?"

"You'll see." He winked at her—*tease*—and his lips curved into a youthful smile that lightened his face. "Are you working?"

"Not at the bar. But I'm tattooing until eight."

"Great. Meet me at the Met at nine."

"The opera?"

"No. The museum."

"But it's closed then." She ought to know. She'd been there enough, had been anticipating the new Matisse exhibit that was finally opening. The Met was one of her go-to places when she needed to escape. There, in the hushed tones of the galleries, surrounded by masterpieces of Botticelli, Monet and van Gogh, she could be alone with her thoughts, put things in perspective, find inspiration for her own work.

Or try to.

"Trust me." Gabe pulled the door open. "It's a surprise."

Devin wrinkled her nose. "I hate surprises."

"You'll like this one, sweet Juliet." He made an over-exaggerated bow. "'Parting is such sweet sorrow, that I shall say good-night till it be morrow.'"

With a final flourish and one last wink, Romeo righted himself and swept out the door. Devin sank to the floor and watched the door swing shut, cutting off her view of his biteable ass in his impeccably tailored pants.

Damn. The man even made a suit look good. Which was saying a lot, coming from her. She usually went for the T-shirt and jeans type. Bad boys who rode motorcycles and smoked clove cigarettes. Probably because they never asked for more than a few laughs and some between-the-sheets action.

Not like Gabe.

Devin dragged her own sorry ass up off the floor. She had three days to figure out what to do about Mr. All-or-Nothing. But first…

She gathered up her boots, tossed them into the closet and flopped onto the sofa. Tucking her feet underneath her, she reached over to the end table and opened the drawer. A ragged stuffed armadillo stared at her with his single, lonely eye, his tail hanging by a thread. She moved it aside and pulled out a spiral notebook with Victor's name scrawled across the faded green cover. Flipping it open, she ran her finger down the page.

Alpine Learning Center.

Institute for Community Living.

Adult Autism Partnership Program.

Pages and pages of institutions, group homes and residential facilities, and next to each one a phone number. She'd dialed them all before. Some more than once.

Nausea churned in her stomach at the thought of starting all over. But Victor needed her. And she was out of options.

First thing tomorrow morning, it was time to start dialing again.

10

"GABE?"

Gabe stood leaning against the base of one of the Met's majestic columns. A guy in a dark blue security-guard uniform who matched the description Noelle had given him—midsixties, slim, with Coke-bottle glasses and white-blond hair—jogged up the steps to meet him. "Gabe Nelson?"

Gabe held out his hand. "You must be Ed. Thanks so much for doing this. It'll mean a lot to my friend." He hoped.

Ed gave the proffered hand a hearty shake. "Well, your sister knows folks in high places. It's not every day the chairman of the board of trustees calls to tell me to open the doors after hours for a prima ballerina's brother and his girl."

"Yeah." Gabe tried to ignore the way his heart lurched at the words *his girl* and focused on the rest of Ed's statement. Gabe had some powerful friends, for sure, but Noelle was on a whole other level. "I owe her one." Or ten. "Did you get the stuff she dropped by for me?"

"It's all set up in the last gallery, like she requested." Ed checked his watch. "Where's your girl? We need to get rolling if you're going to be out of here before I have to make my rounds."

"She should be here any minute." Gabe scanned the

street. Not a raven-haired, long-limbed, tattooed goddess in sight. He'd texted her this morning but hadn't heard back. Maybe he should have arranged to pick her up.

"Tell you what." Ed took his wallet from his pants pocket, pulled out a business card and handed it to Gabe. "Here's my cell number. When she gets here, go around to the entrance at Eighty-First Street and give me a call."

Gabe thanked him again, tucked the card in his shirt pocket and settled back against the column to wait. He was taking a big risk with this stunt, he knew. But great rewards didn't come without great risk. And he had a feeling getting Devin to open up to him might be the greatest reward of all.

"Come here often?"

Devin's voice sounded strained and breathy, like she'd run all the way from Washington Heights. Which wasn't likely in her micro-mini dress and skyscraper heels. Damn, the woman knew how to dress for maximum cock-swelling effect.

He cleared his throat and offered his arm to her, praying she wouldn't notice the reaction under his zipper. This night wasn't about sexual gratification. It was about making a different, deeper connection. "Only when I'm waiting on a beautiful woman. Come on. We're late."

She wrapped a hand around his biceps and they descended the grand staircase, her stilettos clacking on the granite. "I'm sorry. The six train was delayed. Some drunken idiot made a scene and the transit cops had to haul him away."

"You and your subway," he joked, rounding the corner at the end of the stairs.

"You and your cabs," she shot back, her come-hither smile taking any sting out of her words. "So where are we going?"

"Patience, grasshopper." He returned her smile with a

grin that he hoped read boyishly charming and not crazed serial killer. "All will soon be revealed."

They stopped in front of the Eighty-First Street entrance, and he pulled out his cell phone and Ed's business card.

She pursed her lips. "I told you, the museum's closed."

"Trust me." He dialed Ed's number, and Ed picked up on the first ring.

"Ferguson."

"It's Gabe Nelson. We're at the south entrance."

"Great. Be there in five."

Gabe ended the call and stashed the card and cell in his pants pocket.

"Who was that?"

"Friend of a friend."

"On the inside?" She eyed the building as if it was Willy Wonka's chocolate factory and she was Charlie Bucket.

He chuckled. "You make it sound like we're going to raid the joint."

"Aren't we?" She braced one palm against the side of the building, lifted her foot and took off her shoe. "There's a blank wall over my couch just screaming for an original Renoir."

"Don't you mean over your bed?"

"Same diff." She tipped her shoe upside down and shook it. A rock about the size of a pea clattered to the concrete walkway. "Damn. No wonder I could barely walk."

"I thought that was because of the five-inch daggers sticking out of the soles." His balls tightened as she rubbed her foot and let out a low moan, and he had to bite back an answering groan, reminding himself yet again that, no matter how goddamned much he wanted her, he wasn't going to have her. Not until he could convince her this thing between them went way beyond sex. "I don't know how women wear those things. Or why."

"Don't you?" She slipped her shoe back on. "They call them fuck-me pumps for a reason."

Damn. He swallowed hard. Looked as if his resolve was going to get one hell of a workout tonight.

The door creaked open—*hallelujah*—and Ed stood smiling, a shock of snowy hair flopping over one eyebrow.

"Hello, there. I see you found your girl." He appraised Devin in a way that somehow managed to be appreciative without crossing into disrespectful. "Definitely worth waiting for."

"Devin." She stuck out her hand.

"Ed. Pleasure to meet you." He took her hand and kissed it, then let it fall. "We'd better get moving. It'll take you a couple of hours to see the whole exhibit."

"Exhibit?" She studied him suspiciously.

"The Matisse exhibit." Ed stepped back to let them in.

Devin hesitated at the threshold, Gabe right behind her. "But it's not open yet."

"Not to the general public." Ed waved them in. "Follow me."

Devin turned to Gabe, her expression surprised and confused. "How?"

Gabe's chest puffed up. He'd put that look there. Flapped the unflappable Devin Padilla. With a hand on her back, he guided her inside. "A magician never tells his secrets."

"Then…why?"

"Now *that* I can answer." His hand drifted up to her shoulder. "Because you love art. Because you work two jobs and spend your spare time reading to needy kids, and it's time someone did something for you for a change."

She stumbled, and Gabe could have sworn she blinked

back a tear as he steadied her so she could regain her foot-ing. They reached the entrance to the exhibit, and Ed un-hooked a velvet rope. "It's all yours, kids. Enjoy. I'll be back to close up in a couple of hours."

They wandered through the exhibit, taking in paint-ings and paper cut-outs, still life and anatomically cor-rect nudes. All in wild, expressive, often dissonant colors. Devin was alternatively talkative and taciturn, sometimes explaining the artist's work in enthusiastic detail, at other times a still, silent, serious observer.

When they stepped into the last gallery, she stopped short. "What's this?"

"A little refreshment." He crossed to the center of the room, where a red-and-white checkered blanket was spread out on the floor. On it sat a picnic basket, two wine glasses, a bottle chilling in a stainless steel bucket and a crystal vase filled with fresh-cut flowers.

Noelle had outdone herself this time. He really did owe her.

Gabe sat and motioned for Devin to join him. "I don't know about you, but appreciating fine art always makes me hungry."

For what, he didn't say.

She stood, gaping at him. "Are you for real?"

"As real as it gets." He patted the blanket next to him.

"Seriously. You're not like any guy I've ever known."

"Exactly." He opened the basket and started pulling stuff out. Crackers. Brie. Assorted fruit. Some kind of dip and pita chips.

Devin took a few tentative steps toward him and low-ered herself to the blanket. "Seeing as you went through so much trouble, I guess we shouldn't let it go to waste."

Gabe flinched, her words like a punch to his solar plexus. She'd screw him in a heartbeat, no questions asked. But breaking bread with him? That was another story.

A story he was determined to rewrite.

"Strawberry?" He peeled the lid off a plastic container, plucked out a berry and held it out to her.

"Thanks." She bit into it, her lips brushing his fingers for a second until she pulled back, closing her eyes as she chewed. "Mmm."

"That wasn't so bad, was it?"

She shook her head and her lashes fluttered open. A rivulet of juice ran down her chin and he fisted the blanket, resisting the urge to lick the sweet syrup off. "No one's ever fed me before."

"No one's ever done a lot of things for you. But I'd like to change that. If you'll let me." He wiped the droplet away with his forefinger, slid it between his lips and sucked it clean. "Delicious."

"You don't have to work this hard, you know. I'm a safe bet. It's pretty much a given I'll sleep with you." She took another strawberry and popped it into her mouth.

"I told you, I'm not interested in sex."

She raised an eyebrow at him.

"Not just sex."

"I was hoping you changed your mind."

"No such luck."

Without warning, she straddled his lap, knocking over the fruit and crushing the box of crackers with her knee. "Then I guess I'll have to change it for you."

DEVIN FRAMED GABE's face with her hands, his five-o'clock shadow scraping seductively against her palms.

"How's this?" She ground into him, his growing erection pressing into her core. "Changed your mind yet?"

Gabe clamped his hands on her hips, freezing her. "You're doing it again."

"Doing what?" She ran her hands down his chest, loving how his muscles bunched and flexed under the soft cotton of his button-down shirt.

"Using sex to distract me."

"Is it working?" She nudged his collar aside with her nose and pressed her lips to the hollow where his neck met his shoulder. Her tongue darted out for a taste. Clean. Salty. Male.

"There's nothing I'd like more than to bury myself inside you," he growled.

"What's stopping you?" she murmured against his neck. Her tongue stole out for another sample.

"You." He leaned back on his elbows. "What are you so afraid of?"

She shook her head. "I'm not."

"You are." His slate-gray eyes bored into her, and for a second she felt like one of his defendants on the witness stand. "You're afraid to trust me."

She met his gaze head on. "My track record in the trust department is piss poor."

His eyes softened and the hint of a smile played around the corners of his mouth. "I'm not like any of the other guys you've dated. You said so yourself."

She took a deep breath and let it out slowly, shakily. "That's not fair."

"What?" He brushed her hair back and his hand lingered on her cheek, one finger tracing the shell of her ear.

"Doing…that. And using my own words against me."

He laughed, low and sexy. "All's fair in love and war."

"Which is this?" she asked, her voice barely a whisper.

"Both."

The hand on her cheek slid to the back of her head and he drew her in closer, until his lips barely brushed hers. He nibbled her bottom lip then licked it, tracing the seam of her mouth with his tongue. She wound her arms around his neck, trying to hold him tighter to her, force him to deepen this kiss. But he held back, his lips teasing, taunting, refusing to give her more than a hint of what was in store if she gave in to him.

Damn. She might be on top, but he was in control. Again.

"Ready to say uncle?" he asked when he came up for air, his mouth still mere inches from hers.

"What if I am?"

"Then we can take this back to my place, out of range of any security cameras." He gave her another quick kiss, laced with promise. "Have a little faith in me, Devin. In us."

"I don't know how."

"Yes, you do." He rested his forehead against hers. "I won't hurt you. I promise."

She closed her eyes and breathed him in. "You can't promise that. No one can."

"I can promise I won't deliberately hurt you." He raised his head to pierce her again with those stormy eyes. "And if I hurt you unintentionally, I'll do everything in my power to make it right."

"Why me?"

"Why not you?"

"I'm serious, Gabe." She rolled off him and sat on the blanket next to him, putting a good six inches between them. She couldn't think straight when he touched her like that, and thinking straight was an absolute necessity where Gabe was concerned. "I'm a train wreck. I like my skirts too short, my music too loud, my cars too fast. You could have your pick of women with more class in their raised pinkie fingers than I have in my whole body. Women who'll fit in with your crowd, who'll be a political asset instead of a liability."

"Been there, done that. I don't want a running mate. I want a partner. Someone who makes me a better man. And that's you. You've taught me how to stop and smell the pretzels. Helped me become more laid-back. Less stressed. Less—dare I say—boring." He took her hand and turned it over, drawing lazy circles in her palm with his thumb. "Don't desert me now, just when things are getting interesting."

"They are?" The words escaped on a thin breath. Christ, she sounded like a porn star. Or a phone-sex operator.

"Oh, yeah." He brought her palm to his mouth for a kiss.

She shuddered and tried to pull her hand away, but he held fast.

That was the thing about Gabe, she realized, as his thumb went back to work on her palm. He held on to what was important to him with an iron grip. His job. His family.

Her.

Steady. That was the word she'd used to describe him on their walk home from Naboombu. He wasn't a man who would abandon her like her father had. Or neglect her like her mother. He was a man who cherished the people he cared about. And for some unfathomable reason, he cared about her. She'd be an idiot to turn her back on that.

And like Leo always said, she might be *terca como una mula*—as stubborn as a mule—but she was no *pendeja*—dumbass.

"Okay," she whispered after what seemed like an eternity. "Uncle."

"So you trust me?" He twined his fingers with hers and squeezed.

"Yes." She squeezed back.

He shifted his weight so they were touching from

shoulder to fingertip. His breath tickled her ear. "And you admit this isn't just physical? That there's something special between us?"

"Yes." She tilted her head, bringing his mouth in contact with the sensitive spot just below her earlobe. "Now can we get out of here?"

She was practically begging. Not that she cared. She had a few "special" ideas of her own for the rest of their evening, most of which would get them arrested if they tried them at the Met.

"What's wrong?" His lips vibrated against her neck. "You didn't like your private tour?"

"I loved it. It was perfect. But now I want something more private. You know." With her free hand, she reached across and fingered his belt buckle. "So we can concentrate on all that physical stuff you keep talking about."

"You don't have to tell me twice." He stood, pulling her up with him.

"What about all this?" She gestured toward the remains of their aborted picnic.

"My sister will take care of it. She helped me set everything up."

"Holly?" Devin jerked away from him. "I thought she was still in Istanbul."

"She is. I meant Noelle." Gabe tipped his head to study her. "Would it bother you if Holly knew about us?"

Devin bit her lip, her brows knotted in thought. Holly might not like the idea of her best friend and her baby brother getting it on. But she wasn't the kind of person who'd judge them for it. "I guess not. As long as it doesn't bother you."

"Not one damn bit. We're both consenting adults. Right?" He snaked a hand around her waist, tugging her back to him.

"Right." She relaxed against his side.

They walked toward the exit, a shit-eating grin splitting Gabe's handsome face. "So let's get to the consenting part and worry about how my big sister's going to react later."

Outside the building, Gabe whistled for a cab and pulled out his phone.

"Who are you calling?"

"I'm texting Ed and Noelle to let them know we're done here."

A taxi screeched up to the curb. Gabe opened the door, ushered her in and gave the cabbie his address.

"Wait." Devin addressed the driver then turned to Gabe, an idea percolating. She had a way to prove she was serious about trusting him, that as much as she wanted to get him alone where he could screw her in every yoga position imaginable without the threat of jail time, she was willing to open up. At least a little bit. There were parts of her life she'd never shared with anyone else. "Let's go to my place."

"Your place?" Gabe pulled the cab door shut behind him. "I thought you wanted to try out my not-quite-California king? We won't have to fold it up in the morning."

"I do. Some other time." She scooted next to him, ducking under his arm and surrounding herself with his strength, his heat. "Tonight there's something I want to show you."

His eyes sparked with desire. "Everything I want to see is right in front of me."

"You will, believe me. But this is something else. Something in my apartment." She rested her head on his chest. The even rhythm of his heartbeat calmed her, preparing her for the giant leap she was about to take. "My paintings."

"Where to, folks?" the cab driver barked. "I haven't got all night."

"You heard the lady." Gabe's arm tightened around Devin, drawing her impossibly closer to his side. "Her place."

11

"WHAT DO YOU want to see first?" Devin asked the minute the door closed behind them. "Me or my art?"

She was already breathing heavy—hopefully in anticipation of a night of hot, steamy sex and not with exhaustion from their dash up the stairs to her fifth-floor walk-up. Gabe's gaze fell to the shadowy area between her breasts as they rose and fell under the scooped neckline of her dress. "I'd like to be noble enough to say I'm more interested in your artwork than your body. But I'm not sure I can wait that long to touch you."

"That's okay." She pushed him against the door and worked one leg between his, rubbing against him and creating a delicious pressure in his khakis. "I'm not sure I can, either."

"Thank God."

He spun her around so their positions were reversed, her back to the door, his thigh wedged between hers, her full breasts crushed against his torso.

"No fair. I wanted to—"

He cut her off, covering her mouth with his. She made a little mewling sound that hit him deep in his chest and sent ripples of excitement down to his groin. Her lips parted, inviting him to delve deeper, an invitation he didn't hesitate to accept. His tongue swept her mouth from corner to corner before diving in and exploring. His hands roamed over her shoulders, past her waist and down the curve of her lower back, finally settling on the firm globes of her ass.

"Damn." Ever the fucking gentleman, he broke off the kiss before he lost all self-control. "I wanted to go slow. Seduce you."

"Seduce me later." She hooked one leg around his hip and rocked against him. "Fuck me now."

With a groan, he picked her up and carried her to the already folded-out bed. She hitched up her other leg and locked her ankles together behind his back, wrapping her arms around his neck.

"Lazy?" He stopped at the foot of the bed, one side of his mouth twitching upward into a bemused smile. "Or optimistic?"

She tunneled her hands through his hair. "You're not the only one who knows the Boy Scout motto."

"So you're always prepared." His smile spread and he squeezed her glorious ass. "Are you prepared for this?"

He dropped her onto the bed with a gentle bounce and followed her down, draping his body over hers.

"I'd be more prepared if I was naked." She kicked off her shoes, sending them skidding across the floorboards.

"That can be arranged." He propped himself up on one elbow and reached for the hem of her dress with his free hand, inching it upward.

"You, too." She undid one of his shirt buttons.

"Naturally."

They stripped each other quickly, ripping their clothes off without fanfare.

"It's like opening a present," he said, looking down at her. "And it's not even Christmas."

"I'll bet you tore off the wrapping then, too."

"Nope. I was the kid who folded the paper and saved

it to reuse." He traced his fingertips along her collarbone and she rewarded him with a shiver.

Her eyes darted to her leopard thong, in shreds on the floor. "I won't be reusing that any time soon."

"I'll buy you a new one." His lips followed the trail blazed by his fingers. "More than one."

She smoothed a hand down his chest to his abs, coming to rest just below his belly button, within tantalizing reach of his still hardening cock. "Or I could just stop wearing underwear altogether. Save you the trouble of destroying them."

"It's no trouble at all, I assure you."

His mouth claimed hers, letting her know in no uncertain terms that, while he enjoyed witty sex banter as much as the next guy, the time for talking was past. He moved over her and she arched to meet him, twining one slim, strong leg around his and tugging him close.

"Please," she moaned against his mouth, lifting her hips so that the tip of his erection, already wet with precome, brushed her equally slick folds.

Fuck. She felt so damned good beneath him, the perfect combination of strength and softness, round curves and lean muscle. It took all his restraint not to bury himself inside her.

"Condom." He raised his head and searched for his discarded pants, mentally congratulating himself for remembering to slip a fresh Trojan in his wallet before leaving for work that morning.

"I'm on the pill." She pulled his head back down. "And I'm clean."

"I am, too." He took a dusky nipple into his mouth and gave it a quick, teasing swipe with his tongue before releasing it. "Clean, that is."

"I trust you." She gazed up at him, her eyes narrowed with lust. "I want to feel you. Only you."

He dropped his head back and groaned low in his throat as he entered her, feeling her legs wrap around his waist, her heels digging into his back. Shifting so he could go even deeper.

"Oh, *yes*." She clutched his shoulders, urging him to go faster, harder. Only too happy to oblige, he picked up the pace, thrusting into her with short, stabbing strokes.

"Can't hold out much longer," he panted. She was too hot, too tight, too sweet.

"Then don't." She met him thrust for thrust, her heat melding with his steel.

"Come with me." He lowered his head to the valley between her breasts, licking a path to one nipple and sucking it into the warm wetness of his mouth.

"So close."

"Yes."

"Now."

"Please."

Her body shuddered and she ground against him, her fingernails pressing half circles into his back as she climaxed, shouting his name. With one last, powerful thrust he joined her a few seconds later.

Sweat-soaked, Gabe flopped forward.

"You're squashing me." Devin squirmed underneath him. Impossibly, he felt himself hardening all over again inside her.

"Sorry." He started to roll away.

"Don't be." Her arms tightened around him. "I like it."

"I'm not hurting you?" He propped himself up on his elbows.

"Not hurting." Her voice was slurred, her body starting to slacken. "Healing."

Her eyes drifted shut and her breathing evened. He stared down at her, more relaxed in sleep than he'd ever seen her, with her lips slightly parted and her long, ebony lashes resting like wispy shadows against her delicate cheeks. A low moan escaped her as she stretched under him like a cat, and he felt a strange, unfamiliar stirring in the region of his heart.

And that's when he knew.

He wasn't healing her. She was healing him.

"WHAT ABOUT THIS ONE?" Gabe crossed the room to flip around another canvas, rewarding Devin with a spectacular view of his tight ass. Damn, the man was fine. And remarkably unself-conscious in his nudity as he ambled about her apartment. Looked like Operation Loosey Goosey was paying off. "It's different from the rest."

A knot tightened in her belly as she stared at the canvas. She sat up and pulled the sheet to her chin, concealing her bare breasts, as if she could disappear.

Gabe was right. Like the old *Sesame Street* song, that one painting was most definitely not like her others. She usually painted nudes. Some representational, some abstract. Studies of the human form, in all its beauty, with all its imperfections.

A shaft of morning sunlight cut across the canvas Gabe had chosen, bisecting its subject—a stuffed armadillo, love-worn, with an eye missing and his tail dangling by a thread.

Victor's armadillo. Tex.

Telling Gabe about the painting meant telling him the truth, the whole truth and nothing but the truth about her shitty childhood. Exposing a wound she hadn't uncovered since high school. But in a moment of weakness, she'd promised him—and herself—that she'd let him inside her, not just her body but her soul. Maybe even her heart.

"That was Victor's favorite stuffy," she whispered. Her fingers clenched around the sheet. "Tex. He loved that disgusting thing. Wouldn't go anywhere without it. When our last foster family sent him back, it got left behind. I've always wondered how he managed without it."

Gabe leaned the painting back against the wall, face out this time so Tex's one eye was staring at her, and strode to the foot of the bed, where his boxer briefs lay on the floor. "Sent him back?"

"Victor was…difficult. They couldn't handle him. The social worker said she'd try to find a place that would take us both, but…" She looked down at her lap. "I never saw him after that."

"Maybe his adoptive parents bought him a new one." Gabe scooped up his boxers, stepped into them and sat beside her, putting a hand on her thigh.

"Maybe." She focused on the warmth of his hand bleeding through the sheet, calming her, helping her form the words she knew she'd have to say. Fuck, this was hard. "But it wouldn't have been the same. Victor was really attached to Tex."

"I know what you mean. Holly had this nappy fleece blanket she carried everywhere until second grade. She wailed whenever someone tried to take it from her."

"I'm sure she'll appreciate you sharing that with me." Devin lifted her head and met his soft gray eyes, wide with anxiety. "But imagine that times ten."

"That bad?"

"That bad." She took a deep breath, put a hand over his and plunged on. "Autistic kids can develop an unusual attachment to certain toys or books or stuffed animals."

"Autistic?"

She nodded, swallowing. "Victor was diagnosed when he was two and a half."

"That's why finding him is so important to you." He turned his hand over to squeeze hers, lacing their fingers together in that way he had, the way that made her feel as if she was the center of his universe.

"You don't understand." Her bottom lip trembled and she fought to control it. She might be about to spill her secrets, but she wasn't ready to let him see her get all upset and emotional. Crying was for kids, and Devin hadn't been a kid for a long, long time. "It's my fault we got separated. I promised I'd take care of him. And I did until that social worker took him away."

"How old were you? Ten? Twelve?"

"Thirteen."

"You were just a child. Protecting him wasn't your responsibility. That's what adults are for."

"Yeah, well, Victor and I drew the short straw in the adult department."

"Your parents…?"

She relaxed her death grip on the sheet. "My so-called dad took off when Victor was diagnosed. My mom couldn't deal with the pressure of raising us alone. She started using when I was seven."

Gabe didn't say a word, just gathered her to him, his warm, male scent enveloping her. The simple gesture opened a floodgate inside her, words spilling through like blood from a freshly cut artery.

"Pot. Heroin. Crack. Whatever she could get her hands on. I'd catch her shooting up in the bathroom. Got rid of her needles so Victor wouldn't hurt himself. Stole food from the bodega on the corner so we wouldn't go hungry. Which we did anyway."

He swore under his breath. "I wish you had told me sooner."

She froze and he swore again. "That didn't come out right. It's just if I had known what you went through I could have…I don't know. Done…something."

"What's the point?" She squeezed her eyes shut as the tension drained from her muscles. "The past is past."

"The point is you shouldn't have to bear that kind of burden alone. There are people in your life—me, Holly, Leo—who you can lean on."

"I'm not so great at the whole leaning thing."

"I can see that. Fortunately, I've got really broad shoulders. Perfect for leaning on."

She opened her eyes to find him peering down at her, his gaze an alluring mix of concern and heat. Her heart did a little tap dance.

"Tell you what." He stroked a finger down her arm. "How about we get dressed and head out for some breakfast?"

"I've got a better idea." She took his hand and moved it to her breast. "The deli on the next block delivers, and they've got the best country ham, egg and cheese croissant south of Houston Street. Then we can spend the day in bed. Undressed."

"Sounds great." He cupped one plump mound through the sheet and squeezed. "Mind if I use your shower? Dressed or not, I stink."

She pressed her nose to his chest and inhaled. "I like the way you smell. Sweaty, like a real man. But help yourself. I'll join you once I've ordered the food."

He gave her a quick kiss and headed to the bathroom, giving her another chance to ogle him from behind. When he'd closed the door and she'd stopped drooling, she dropped the sheet and scrambled for her cell phone.

"Hey, Mateo. It's Devin. Can I have two of the usual and a couple of large French roasts, black? With milk and sugar on the side," she added at the last minute, realizing she had no clue how Gabe took his coffee.

"Two?" Mateo's surprised voice crackled over the line. "You must be *mucha hambre* this morning."

"Damn skippy. How fast can you get here?"

"Fifteen minutes. Twenty, tops."

"Thanks, *bonito*."

She ended the call, tossed her phone on the bed next to her and swung her feet onto the floor. The sound of running water told her Gabe was already in the shower, and she licked her lips at the thought of his magnificent, wet nakedness, slick and soapy, ready to play.

Oh, yeah.

She was about to ditch the sheet in favor of some smexy shower action when someone pounded on the door.

Shit.

No way was that Mateo so quickly. Either someone had the wrong apartment or one of her neighbors needed to borrow something.

"Hang on," she called. "I'll be right there."

She threw on a tank top and shorts, not bothering with anything underneath, and answered the door.

"Surprise!"

Holly wrapped Devin in a bear hug, her just-showing baby bump grazing Devin's stomach.

"You're home." Devin cast a panicked glance around the apartment, her eyes falling on Gabe's khakis in a heap by the television, his shirt hanging over the bookshelf, one of his shoes peeking out from under the bed. "Early."

Holly released her and brushed past through the door. "Nick finished filming ahead of schedule."

"Where is your handsome husband?" Devin followed, kicking the offending khakis behind the TV and stuffing the shirt between two books. "You're usually inseparable. Nauseatingly so."

"His agent's in town. They're meeting at Pastis for a business breakfast, and I've been meaning to return my spare key to the super." Holly sank into the armchair in the corner. "Man, I'm beat. I don't even want to think about what this little bugger's going to do to me in the third trimester."

Holly toed off her espadrilles and lifted one foot to massage the arch, and Devin groaned inwardly. She'd never get her friend out now. And it was only a matter of time before Holly noticed the water running in the bathroom. Or Gabe's loafer, which Devin couldn't shove under the bed now without rousing suspicion.

Her only option was to come clean, admit she had a guy stashed in the can and get Holly out the door before she figured out it was Gabe. Not that she was embarrassed, but this was so not how she wanted Holly to find out she was boffing her brother.

"Listen, Holls, I'm dying to catch up with you, but I'm kind of in the middle of something right now." She eyed the bathroom door. As if on cue, the water stopped.

"Ohmigod, you've got a man in there." Holly squealed. "I can't believe it. The love-'em-and-kick-'em-to-the-curb queen actually let a guy spend the night. Who is it?"

"Just…a guy. We're keeping it on the down-low."

"Oh, please," Holly huffed. "As I recall you practically shouted to an entire coffee shop that I was doing Nick."

"I promise I'll tell you. Let me deal with him and I'll meet you at the deli up the block in ten." Maybe she could intercept Mateo on the way over and grab her sandwich and coffee.

"Fine, be that way." Holly slipped on her espadrilles and stood, rubbing her belly. "For now. But I'm warning you, I want to meet this paragon who got you to break your no-sleepovers rule. Soon."

As though they were living in a bad sitcom, the bathroom door creaked open and Gabe stepped out, his hair still wet from the shower and a towel fastened around his waist.

"I heard voices. Is breakfast here?"

"Gabe?" Holly's mouth fell open and she pressed a hand to her chest.

"Holly." He hiked up the towel, which had slipped to his hips. "You're supposed to be in Istanbul."

Devin shrugged a shoulder and gave her friend a wry smile.

"Surprise."

12

"Sorry I'm late." Devin slid into the seat across from Holly at the café table, plunking down her French roast and unwrapping her sandwich. She'd showered and changed in record time, but as hungry as she was, she wasn't about to miss out on breakfast. Plus, she didn't want to stick Gabe with the tab. Her place. Her treat. "I couldn't leave without..."

"Please." Holly held up a hand, palm out. "Spare me the intimate details of your sex life with my brother."

"As if I'd share that." Devin crossed one leg over the other and adjusted the hem of her shorts. "I was going to say I had to intercept the delivery guy with my croissant, but whatever."

"Don't 'whatever' me." Holly sipped her iced chai latte—decaf, Devin was sure, given Holly's current state. "You know what they say about payback. Remember when you made Gabe drive all the way to Connecticut so you could interrogate me about Nick? It's my turn to give you the third degree."

Oh, yeah, Devin remembered, all right. Two and a half hours in a car with Gabe. She'd always found him attractive, but that trip was when she'd really become aware of him as a man. His thigh had been inches from hers for the duration, his scent surrounding her.

Christ, it had been fun needling him. And man, oh, man, was he hot when he was bothered.

Not that she was confessing any of that to his sister.

"I'm an open book," Devin bluffed, taking a hit of strong coffee. "What do you want to know?"

"You can start with how you and Gabe went from loathing to lovey-dovey in the little time I've been gone."

Devin averted her eyes, staring at a cheap framed poster on the opposite wall with the slogan Coffee Solves Everything in bold red letters. If only it did. "I wouldn't exactly call us lovey-dovey."

"Then what would you call it?"

"We're—" Devin paused, not exactly sure what they were. More than fuck buddies, but not quite lovers "—getting to know each other."

"Looked like you knew each other pretty well to me."

Devin's attention snapped back to her friend. "I didn't mean physically. Obviously, we've crossed that bridge."

"TMI." Holly blushed and shook her head, sending her brown bob flying. "I'm sorry. That was snarky. It's just… he's my baby brother. And he's coming off a bad breakup. I don't want to see him get hurt again."

"You mean Kara?" Devin took a bite of her sandwich, savoring the buttery, cheesy goodness.

Holly nodded. "I helped him pick out the ring, thanks to email and Skype."

Devin coughed, almost spewing croissant across the table. "Ring?"

Holly went on like she didn't notice Devin was three seconds from needing the Heimlich maneuver.

"Two carats, emerald cut. Not my style." She waved her hand, flashing a simple white-gold band with a small, bezel-set diamond. "But from what Gabe told me, definitely Kara's speed."

"I didn't realize they were that serious." Devin gulped

her coffee. It scalded her throat but even that didn't dull the shock of Holly's news.

"Oh, crap." Holly buried her face in her hands. "Me and my big mouth. I should have figured my tight-lipped brother wouldn't say anything."

"Don't stop now." Devin leaned back and crossed her arms. "She turned him down?"

Holly's words were muffled through her fingers. "I don't know what happened. He just told me it didn't work out."

"When?"

"When what?"

"When did he tell you?"

"A couple of weeks ago, I guess." Holly lifted her head. "About a month after Nick and I arrived in Istanbul."

Shit. A couple of weeks. Right around the time he'd found her in the park with Fast Fingers Freddie.

"He didn't say why they broke up?" Devin cringed. She sounded like a fucking teenage girl.

"Only that the relationship had run its course." Holly added another creamer to her latte and stirred. "Something about Kara being bored with him."

Gabe's words on the cab ride home and on Devin's doorstep that night came rushing back at her.

Do you think I'm boring? How's this for boring?

"She didn't deserve him," Devin snapped with more intensity than she intended.

"I know. Gabe brought her to see *The Lesser Vessel* and Nick and I met them afterward for drinks. She told me my nails were a mess, my skin was ashy and my hair was 'holding me back.'" Holly put air quotes around the last three words. "From what I don't know. But Gabe loved her. Or at least he thought he did. It couldn't have been easy for him having his proposal thrown back in his face."

Do you think I'm boring? How's this for boring?

"No. It wasn't."

"So you can see why I'm worried about him jumping into another relationship."

Was that what they had? A relationship? Not much of one if Gabe wasn't willing to be up front with her, especially after he'd pushed her to reveal her demons.

"Look, your brother and I are hanging out. Having fun. Neither one of us wants anything complicated."

Devin's heart cracked a little more with each word. Damn, she'd really been starting to fall for the guy. Served her right for trusting someone. Even someone as basically decent as Gabe. Because in the end, everyone left.

Everyone.

She fought the urge to lash out, not at him but at her own stupidity. For one brief, insane moment she'd forgotten the lyrics inscribed on her wrist. She looked down at them, the script blurring.

Not afraid to walk this world alone.

"Are you sure?" Holly's voice, tinged with worry, broke through the haze.

"Is a whiskey sour sour?" Devin unfolded her arms and rested them on the table. "You okay with this?"

"Do I have a choice?" Holly shrugged. "Seriously, the last time I checked you're both over eighteen. Free to do what you want. I admit I'm surprised, but I can't say I'm opposed."

"Thanks, I guess."

Holly reached across the table and covered Devin's hand with her own. "I love you both. You know that. I just don't want either one of you to get your heart broken."

Too late for that.

Devin's cell chimed and she grabbed it from her purse. She swiped the screen and saw a text had come through.

"Gabe?" Holly arched a brow over the rim of her cup.

"Mmm-hmm." Devin tapped the screen and the message flashed across.

"He's interrupting our girl talk." A frown creased Holly's forehead. "What does he want?"

Devin started to read, her lips moving silently.

Sorry our plans for today got scratched. Make it up to you? Dinner. My place. 8:00. Wear those tall, black boots. I'm dying to—

"Hey!" Devin glared at Holly, who was clutching the stolen phone in one traitorous hand.

"Nothing complicated, huh?" Holly looked down at the screen and read aloud. "Dying to fuck you in them? Sounds pretty complicated to me."

"Give it back." Devin flexed her fingers, ready to snatch the damned thing out of her friend's grasp.

"My brother's a regular Lord Byron." Holly shuddered and handed the phone over.

Devin tossed it into her purse. "That's what you get for reading a private text."

"Point taken." Holly raised her arms in surrender. "Are you working tonight?"

"No." Devin drained her coffee. "But I'm not having dinner with Gabe."

"Why not?"

"You don't want your brother in pieces, do you?" Devin set her empty cup down on the table with a hollow thunk. "Because if I see him tonight, I'm going to rip him a new one."

"One thing marriage to Nick has taught me is that communication is key." Holly took Devin's hand in hers again and squeezed. "Go. Talk to him."

"I'm more of a doer than a talker."

"If my brother wasn't totally honest with you about Kara—"

"He wasn't." Devin wrapped up what was left of her sandwich and chucked it into the garbage can behind her, her appetite suddenly nonexistent.

"—then he must have had a good reason."

"I can't imagine what."

"There's only one way to find out."

Devin groaned, knowing what was coming next.

"Ask him."

THE DOORBELL RANG just as Gabe was about to start making the béchamel sauce for his mother's famous chicken fettuccini Alfredo. He checked the clock above the professional-grade stove.

Seven thirty. Devin was early. Hopefully that meant she was as eager to see him as he was to see her.

"Be right there."

He put the heavy cream, butter and parmesan cheese back in the side-by-side stainless steel fridge, gave the counter a quick wipe down and headed for the door.

"You're early," he said as he flung it open to find her standing there in typical Devin attire—a purple crop top, black leather miniskirt and hot pink combat boots that had him straining against his zipper in seconds. "Not that I'm complaining."

"You might be when you hear what I've got to say." She flounced past him, her purse swinging from one shoulder and almost hitting him in the ass.

So much for being happy to see him.

"Okay." He followed her into the living room. "Let's talk."

"Why didn't you tell me you proposed to Kara?"

His stomach plummeted. She sure as hell didn't waste any time getting to the point.

"Let me guess. Holly let it slip?"

"That doesn't answer my question." She planted herself in the middle of the room with her hands on her hips.

Gabe rubbed a hand over his chin. "I didn't tell you because it wasn't important."

"Wasn't important?" Devin held her arms stiffly at her sides, clenching her hands into tight little balls. "You asked her to spend the rest of her life with you, for Christ's sake."

"That was a mistake."

"Don't you mean kissing me was the mistake?"

"No." He crossed to her and put his hands on her shoulders, grateful she didn't shrink away from him. "Kissing you was the best damn decision I ever made."

"Just answer one question."

"Anything."

"When?" She stared at him, her mouth set, her gaze unwavering.

"When what?" he asked uncertainly.

"When did you propose to her?" She tilted her chin defiantly. "Was it the night you found me and Freddie in the park?"

Shit. She wasn't going to like his answer. But he wasn't going to lie to her. Not after he'd all but forced her to open up to him. "Yes."

"I knew it." She shook his hands off and stepped back, crossing her arms. "I'm your fucking rebound girl. Sloppy seconds."

"That's not true." He moved toward her but she held him off with an outstretched palm.

"What else do you call the girl you hooked up with mere hours after your would-be fiancée dumped your sorry ass?"

"Look, I admit that first kiss was…" A shudder ran through him at the memory of how she'd felt in his arms that night, her tongue dueling with his, the delicious friction of her thigh moving against his hard-on. "Impulsive. I was trying to prove something, mostly to myself. But only at the start."

"Wait, don't tell me." Sarcasm hung from her words like icicles. "The minute your lips met mine birds sang, the earth moved and the angels wept."

"That's not the half of it." He took another step toward her and was relieved when this time she didn't fend him off. "That kiss was the beginning of my end. You destroyed me, sweetheart. I couldn't get you out of my head. If you hadn't walked into my office that day, it was only a matter of time before I came looking for you."

"How am I supposed to believe you?"

"It's called trust. Remember how I said I'd never try to hurt you? And that if I did, I'd do everything in my power to make it right?" One more step and he was able to reach out and take her small, soft hands in his larger ones. Her fingers were surprisingly cold, and he pressed them together and rubbed them for warmth. "This is me. Doing everything in my power to make it right."

He inclined his head toward the mahogany leather sectional against the wall. "Please. Sit down. Let me explain."

Her eyes narrowed and she pulled her hands away.

"Okay." She stalked over to the sofa and sat, crossing her long, bare legs in a slow, sultry way that made his cock twitch. "Explain."

He took a deep breath, willing his uncooperative dick to behave, and sat next to her. Close enough for him to smell her almond shampoo, but not so close that they were touching. That would be like pouring gasoline on a forest fire, and he needed to be operating on all cylinders if he was going to get through this in one piece—with Devin still speaking to him when he was done. "I should have told you about Kara. But I knew the minute—the second—I kissed you that she was all wrong for me."

"You needed a kiss to figure that out?" Devin rolled her eyes. "I could tell just from watching her work the room at the pub crawl."

"What can I say?" In a move he'd been practicing since high school, he eased an arm over the back of the couch. "I'm not as people-savvy as you. But I'm smart enough to realize there was no way I could be right about her and kiss you like that."

"Like what?"

"Like this."

The hand on the back of the sofa dropped down to the nape of her neck, his fingers working through her thick dark hair to caress the skin underneath. He dipped his head, inching toward her.

Her cornflower eyes darkened to a midnight blue as his lips crushed hers. After a brief hesitation, she opened her mouth in welcome and he breathed her in, wanting to inhale her essence, taste every soft, sweet inch of her, indulge in the feel of her lush curves molded to his body.

His tongue circled hers greedily while his free hand snaked around her waist, drawing her closer. A moan erupted from deep in her throat and she collapsed against his chest, surrendering. Desire coursed through his veins and he wanted to pound his chest and roar like some caveman laying claim to his woman.

His woman.

As a warm tingle spread through his body, his head recognized what his heart had known since their first night together.

He was in love with Devin.

He raised his head to stare at her, longing to tell her but knowing it was way too soon. Pushing her too hard, too fast would only make her bolt. Glassy eyes, drunk with passion, met his and his chest swelled with the knowledge that he'd put that look there.

"Damn you," she whispered, pulling his head back down for more.

This time the kiss was slower, sweeter, like a welcome home, a promise of things to come.

"See what I mean?" he asked when they broke apart again. "Definitely not the kiss of a man in love with another woman."

"Point taken." She tucked her legs under her and shifted so that her face nestled in the crook of his neck.

He rested his chin on the top of her head. "As long as we're doing true confessions, there's one more thing I should probably tell you."

"You didn't propose to anyone else, did you?" She trailed a hand down the buttons on his shirt.

"Hardly." He chuckled. "I didn't want to get your hopes up, but I asked my inspector to track down some leads on Victor."

"What kind of leads?" The hand on his chest stilled.

"His last known address. All the hospitals, group homes and residential facilities in the tristate area that take patients with autism."

She sighed. "Been there, done that."

"Murphy's got connections you don't. He can cast a wider net. Dig deeper." And he would. Gabe had made sure of that when he'd called to tell him about Victor's autism.

"Is that legal?" Devin lifted her head and looked at him. "Won't you both get fired for misusing state resources or something?"

"He's doing it off the clock."

"For free?" Her voice started to rise. "How can I repay him?"

This was the part that was really going to piss her off.

Gabe scraped a hand through his hair and charged ahead. "You don't have to. I am."

She tensed in his arms. "Why would you do that?"

"Because that's what friends do. They help each other out."

"Is that what we are?" She pursed her lips. "Friends?"

"I'd like to think so." He kissed her nose. "Isn't that how all good relationships start?"

"I wouldn't know."

"Well, it's about time you found out." He laid a hand over hers, still on his chest, needing her to feel the erratic beating of his heart, to understand without words how much she meant to him. "Let me do this for you. Please."

It seemed like a lifetime went by before she answered.

"Okay." She relaxed almost imperceptibly against him. "But I'm paying you back. I don't know when. I don't know how. But I am."

"I'll tell you how you can start." With his free hand he cupped her face, caressing her cheek. "Come to the New York City Ballet fundraiser with me next week. Noelle's performing."

"That doesn't sound like payback."

"Have you ever been to one of those things? It can be torture."

"I thought you liked the ballet."

"I do. It's the ballet patrons I can't stand."

"Won't the rest of your family be there? You don't need me."

"That's where you're wrong, sweetheart." He slid his hand to her shoulder, one finger toying with the strap on her tank top. "I always need you."

"I don't have anything to wear…" She tipped her head to one side, all but begging him to explore the elegant column of her neck with his lips.

So he did, starting at the spider web tattoo behind her

ear and traveling down to the crest of the phoenix's head on her breast. "Wear whatever you want."

"But the people at those things…"

"Are just people. Say. You'll. Come." He punctuated each word with a kiss on her shoulder, her neck and finally her jaw.

"Now who's distracting who with sex?"

"Not distracting. Persuading." He smiled against her skin. "Is it working?"

She moaned and grabbed his shirt in her fist. "Fuck, yes."

"And you'll go with me?"

She answered by climbing into his lap, taking his face in her hands and soul-kissing him. And it was a long time before he got around to making dinner.

13

"HEY, DEVIN." MANNY POKED his head through the curtain that separated the waiting area of Ink the Heights from the work space. "Some guy's up front with a package for you."

"Tell him to leave it at the desk." She didn't look up from the thigh she was tattooing with an intricate, black-and-white maple tree, complete with roots and leaves, that ran from her client's hip to just above her knee. "I'm busy."

"No can do." Manny clucked his tongue. "He says you need to sign for it."

Devin glanced at the clock. Two fifteen. *Shit*. Less than five hours before she was supposed to meet Gabe at Lincoln Center, and she still had no idea what the fuck she was wearing. Leo had promised she could take off as soon as she finished with this client, but she couldn't afford any interruptions if she wanted to be even halfway presentable for Gabe.

And his family.

And all the muckety-mucks who were certain to be at the benefit.

Shit squared. Maybe even cubed.

She must have been on a precoital high when she agreed to this date. She had no business being at a society event—would probably scare off all the potential donors with her tats and piercings. And her general disdain for the upper crust.

Maybe it wasn't too late to back out. She could always use the tried-and-true headache excuse and hide in her apartment with a family-size bag of chips and season four of *The Walking Dead* on Netflix.

Except running and hiding wasn't Devin's style. She was an in-your-face kind of girl. She was also the kind of girl who kept her promises, and she'd promised both Gabe and Holly she'd be there.

"I can't stop now." She almost laughed out loud at the unintended double meaning of her words. She couldn't stop in the middle of a complex tattoo, and she couldn't stop the wheels that had been set in motion for tonight. She concentrated on outlining a particularly tricky branch. "Sign for me."

"Tried that. Guy wouldn't budge."

"Fine." Devin blew a stray strand of hair off her forehead. "Tell him I'll be out in a minute. I've got to finish this section."

Manny disappeared, and she worked for another few minutes before laying down her needle on her sterile tray and pressing a gauze pad over the freshly inked area. "Okay, Jazmin. Hold that in place and hang tight. I'll be right back."

Devin whipped off her gloves and tossed them into the garbage on her way out to the reception room.

"I hope you're going to tell me I won the Publisher's Clearing House grand prize," she said as she burst through the curtain. "Because nothing short of that is worth the interruption."

"Sorry, no." The delivery man set a long, flat box on the counter and held out a tablet and stylus for her to sign. "But the package is from Bergdorf Goodman, if that's any consolation."

Devin paused midsignature. The super high-end clothing store was definitely not on her shopping radar. Or in her budget. "I didn't order anything from there."

The delivery dude took the tablet from her hands and checked it while the nosy *buscavidas* scattered around the reception area set aside their magazines to watch the unfolding drama.

"Says right here to deliver to Devin Padilla at Ink the Heights, 1443 St. Nicholas Avenue. That's you, right?"

"Right."

"Then sign." He returned the tablet to her.

"But…"

"Oh, wait. I almost forgot." He reached into his inside jacket pocket and pulled out a card. "There's a note, too. Maybe that'll explain everything."

She scrawled her signature and fished a couple of ones out of the tip jar and handed them over, making a mental note to replace them later.

"Thanks." He tucked the tablet under his arm and pocketed the money. With a mock salute for Devin and a nod to the waiting customers, he left.

She stared from the card in her hands to the package on the counter, not sure which to open first.

"Open the card," a middle-aged woman with a full sleeve of tats on her right arm piped up over the June issue of *Inked*. "See who it's from before you decide whether to accept it."

"No way, open the box," another woman disagreed. "Then if you like it you can keep it no matter who gave it to you."

"I say don't open either one," a heavyset man on the other side of the room chimed in. "The whole thing's probably a practical joke. Or a bomb. I read last week a guy in Queens got a letter laced with anthrax."

"Did I ask for opinions from the peanut gallery?"

Devin snatched up the box and took it through the curtain back to her work space to a chorus of disappointed groans, punctuated by a few Spanish curse words.

"Oooh, is that the Bergdorf's logo?" Jazmin craned her neck for a peek as Devin tried unsuccessfully to stash the box unnoticed behind her chair. "What's inside?"

"I don't know." Devin set the box down and fingered the card. Her name was written in a strong, masculine hand on the envelope. "It's a gift. I haven't opened it."

"Well, come on, *muchacha*." Jazmin nudged her with one elbow. "What are you waiting for?"

"I should really get back to work on your ink."

"We can finish up next week. I was starting to get a little sore, anyway." Jazmin lifted the gauze pad and inspected her new tattoo.

"Keep that covered." Devin gave her client a fresh pad and threw the used one into the medical waste container.

"Stop changing the subject." Jazmin pouted. "Open the package."

"Okay, okay." First the waiting room crew, now Jazmin. What was with these people? They took meddling to a whole new level.

Devin tore open the card, knowing whose signature she'd find inside. *Can't wait to see you in this at the ballet tonight. And out of it at my place after. Yours, Gabe.*

Was he? Hers? And she, his? Was that what all this, surprise museum trips and unexpected presents and life-changing orgasms, was adding up to?

Fat chance. Devin crumpled up the card in her fist. He'd pushed her further than any man had before. Gotten her to admit that their relationship—God, she hated that word—went beyond the physical. But belonging to each other? Lifetime commitment? His and hers towels? No way. Forever wasn't in her DNA.

"Who's it from?" Jazmin's voice brought her back to the matter at hand.

"A friend." Devin eyed the box at her feet.

"Must be a good friend if he's shopping for you at Bergdorf's."

"Who says it's a he?"

"The blush creeping up your face." Jazmin waggled a finger at her. "Quit stalling. Let's see what your *novio* picked out for you."

"He's not my…" Devin's denial died in her throat. What was the point? They were seeing each other almost every night. Humping like sex fiends. And now he was sending her expensive gifts. That made Gabe her boyfriend, didn't it? Even if hearing it out loud gave her the willies. "Never mind."

Devin laid the box flat on the floor, knelt beside it and lifted off the lid. She peeled back the mountains of tissue paper and stood, lifting up a stunning beaded mermaid gown in a deep, rich red, with a sweetheart neckline, wide, gathered shoulder straps and an open back.

"Aye, dios mio," Jazmin breathed. "Alexander McQueen."

"You've seen it for all of two seconds. How can you tell the designer?"

"I watch *Project Runway*. And stalk the fashion blogs. That gown is part of his new collection. It's worth over five thousand dollars."

"What?" The gown slipped in Devin's shocked hands, and she clutched it to her chest to stop it from falling into a five-thousand-dollar heap on the floor.

"Exquisite." Leo came up behind her, his voice startling her so she almost dropped the damned thing again. "Your Gabriel has outdone himself."

Devin grimaced. "Shouldn't you be working?" she snapped.

"I just finished up on Hector." Leo stood firmly planted, hands on his hips. "And my next client ran next door to get some cash from the ATM."

Great. A bigger audience.

"Ooh, try it on," Jazmin purred.

Devin draped the dress over her arm. "Not now."

"Look, there's more." Jazmin had gotten down from the chair and was crouched next to the still open box, holding up a pair of matching mesh and suede pumps. "Jimmy Choo."

"You realize these names mean nothing to me, right?"

"Well, they should." Jazmin dangled the shoes from her fingertips. "They mean your *novio* has expensive tastes and the *cuartos* to indulge them."

Devin snatched the shoes in her free hand, tucked the box under her arm and stomped toward the storeroom.

"Square up with Jazmin, and schedule her for a follow-up early next week," she called over her shoulder. "Someone's got some 'splainin' to do."

"Hey, boss. You got a minute?" Murphy stuck his head inside Gabe's office door.

Gabe looked up from his keyboard at his inspector. "I have to file this motion by five. Can it wait?"

"You're going to want to see this." Murphy waved a DVD. "We got the surveillance tapes from the victim's apartment building."

Gabe pushed back his chair and followed Murphy down the hall to the video room, whistling as he went.

"What's with you?" Murphy slowed his steps to let Gabe catch up with him. "You take happy pills or something?"

"Just in a good mood, I guess." Gabe swung open the door marked Video Room. "It's a beautiful day. Birds singing. Flowers blooming. Taxi drivers cutting each other off. What's not to like?"

"Well, I hope this doesn't burst your bubble." Murphy pushed past him and headed straight for the combination TV/DVD player.

"Not likely." Taking a seat at the conference table in the center of the room, Gabe fought a smile. It would take an elephant dart to bring him down today. He checked his watch. In about four and a half hours he'd be with Devin, at the ballet.

"Let me get it cued up." Murphy fiddled with the DVD player. "The interesting part's at around 12:30 p.m."

"That's almost five hours before the medical examiner's estimated time of death."

"Exactly." Murphy's finger hovered over the play button. "Ready?"

"Whenever you are."

Murphy started the DVD. The entrance to the Park Avenue apartment building where the bodies were found popped up on the screen. The angle of the camera caught everyone coming and going. Including a man in jeans, a stained, white T-shirt and a tool belt, swinging a tool box in one arm.

"Pause it." Gabe leaned forward, elbows on the table. "Was that who I think it was?"

"Yep." Murphy crossed his arms in front of his chest. "That's our guy, all right. The defendant. On his way out. Five hours before the murder."

Gabe slumped in his seat. No wonder their witness was wavering. She was wrong.

"I take it there's nothing that shows him returning."

"Nope."

"And no other way in or out of the building."

"Negative."

Gabe tugged at his collar, which all at once seemed to be choking him. "How did we miss this?"

"Problem is—" Murphy cleared his throat "—I don't think we did."

"What do you mean?"

"Remember how we thought the security camera wasn't working?"

"Yeah." Gabe scowled at his inspector, still not following.

"Well, someone from this office watched the video from the day of the murder. He paid off the guard on duty to erase it and say he'd accidentally turned off the camera. But the guard didn't feel right about it, so he saved it onto a USB drive. Just in case."

"If someone bribed him to erase it, why come forward with it now?"

"Because that someone is no longer working the case."

Jack.

"Shit." Gabe slammed his fist on the table. "That unethical little prick. He completely screwed us."

"You said it." Murphy took a step toward Gabe and jammed his hands in his pockets. "We have to disclose this to the defense. We're going to look like assholes."

"Fuck disclosure. We might have to dismiss the whole damn case." Gabe pushed back his chair and stood, the motion he had to file suddenly the least of his concerns. "I've got to talk to Holcomb. Now."

"Before you do, there's something else you should see." Murphy turned back to the DVD player and pressed Fast Forward. The images zoomed past.

"Please tell me it's not more bad news." Although Gabe didn't know how it could get any worse. Withholding evidence that could prove the defendant's innocence was pretty much the lowest a prosecutor could sink.

And this guy wanted to be district attorney?

Over Gabe's dead body.

"Depends on how you look at it." Murphy froze the DVD. "Here we are. 5:25 p.m."

"Right around the time of death."

Murphy nodded and restarted the video. For a few seconds, there wasn't any movement. Then a grainy figure came into the frame. It was a man of average build, his face obscured by a gray hoodie. He paused briefly to adjust something in his pocket then ducked out the door.

"Our murderer?"

"Possibly."

"Not much to go on."

"Forensics is enhancing it and printing up some stills. We're going to recanvass the neighborhood, show them around and see if anyone recognizes him."

"Great." Gabe ran a hand through his hair and headed for the door, continuing to speak as he went. "Get Colby and Renwick to help. I'll clean up Kentfield's mess."

Five minutes later he was on the seventh floor, talking his way past Doris to Holcomb's private sanctuary. This wasn't going to be easy or pleasant, no matter how much he detested Jack. He knocked.

"Come in," Holcomb barked from inside.

Gabe pushed open the door. "I apologize for the interruption…"

"This better be important, Nelson." Holcomb spun around in his desk chair and waved Gabe in. "I've got a press conference in twenty minutes."

"It is, sir. It's about the Park Avenue homicide case." Gabe made sure the door closed behind him before continuing. "We may have the wrong man."

Holcomb jerked upright in his chair, the full force of his razor-sharp attention on Gabe. "What do you mean, 'may have'?"

"The surveillance tapes show the defendant leaving the

scene almost five hours before the murders and another man in a gray hoodie exiting shortly after the medical examiner's estimated time of death."

"Why are we just finding out about this now?"

"Well, that's another issue." Gabe stood taller, determined not to let his boss intimidate him. Hell, he hadn't done anything wrong. It wasn't his fault Jack was a complete douche. Okay, so he was the douche's immediate supervisor, but he couldn't and shouldn't have to watch him 24/7. "The security guard we got the video from says he was paid off to destroy it."

"Paid off? By who?" Holcomb's amber eyes speared Gabe.

Gabe shifted his weight, rocking slightly. "You're not going to like this."

"Cop?"

"Prosecutor." Gabe clasped his hands behind his back. "Kentfield."

"What motive would he have for hiding evidence?" Holcomb tapped a finger thoughtfully against his cheek. "How do we know this security guard is telling the truth?"

"We don't," Gabe admitted. "Yet."

"Then come back when you have some real proof Kentfield was involved."

"And until then?"

"Do what you have to do." Holcomb plucked a pen from a container on his desk and clicked it absently. "Disclose the video. Talk to the security guard. Track down the man in the hoodie."

He pointed the pen at Gabe, piercing him with another stare. "But until we've got another suspect in custody, this handyman's our guy. And he stays in Rikers."

Holcomb turned back to his computer, dismissing Gabe.

With a shake of his head, Gabe started for the door, only to be stopped by one more blast of Holcomb's voice.

"And Gabe."

Gabe froze.

"Until you can prove someone from this office withheld evidence, this stays right here." Holcomb's tone was hard and flat, one Gabe knew from experience brooked no dissent. "I don't want to see this aired out in the press."

"Understood."

Gabe let the door slam shut and rushed for the elevator. Goddamn Holcomb, leaving him hanging out to dry. He should have known the big man wouldn't want to get his hands dirty, even though his term of office was coming to a close. Who knew what kind of sweetheart deal he'd worked out for himself in the private sector.

The elevator dinged at the same time Gabe's cell rang. He stepped in, hit the button for the third floor with the heel of his hand and answered the call, not bothering to check who it was. "Gabe Nel—"

He was cut off by a barrage of Spanish in a familiar female voice. He caught a few words, like *vestido*, *costosa* and *estupido*.

"I take it you got the dress," he finally managed to interject when she took a breath. "What's the matter? Not your color?"

"I'll tell you what's the matter." Her voice seemed to rise an octave with each word. "It's too damn expensive, that's what."

Gabe winced. The dress was too much. He should have known Devin would be insulted by what she'd no doubt view as a hand-out. He'd almost gone with something simpler, more understated. But he made the mistake of texting pictures of the two gowns to his sister, and Holly had convinced him that the rich red beading would look striking against Devin's light mocha skin. And it would, if he could worm his way out of this and convince her to wear it. "It's not a big deal, honest."

"Not a big deal? You call five thousand dollars not a big deal?" He had to hold the phone away from his head. "That's almost three months' rent."

Not for me, Gabe thought. Not that he was dumb enough to make things worse by saying it.

"I appreciate the gesture," Devin continued, her voice a tad calmer. "Really, I do. But I can't accept it. Or the shoes."

The elevator doors slid open and Gabe got off, making way for a frazzled-looking woman with a copy of the *New York Post* under her arm. The paper was folded so that its infamous Page Six gossip section faced outward. Tina Fey and Amy Poehler smiled at him from a picture above the fold, flanking the mayor at some charity event. He snapped his fingers. "I have an idea."

"No."

"You haven't even heard it." He waved to his secretary on his way past and pushed open his office door.

"If it involves me wearing this outfit, I don't have to." A rustling sound crackled over the line, like she was putting the dress back in the box.

"Hear me out." He sank into his chair and propped his feet up on the desk.

The other end of the line went quiet for a minute. "Okay," she said finally. "What's your brilliant idea?"

"Wear the dress and shoes tonight."

"I told you." Her tone spiked again. "There's no way…"

"You didn't let me finish," he interrupted. "Wear them. Hob nob with the elite. Get yourself photographed by the press. I know a guy at the *Post* who can make sure your picture hits the society page. Maybe even get you a mention in Cindy Adams's column."

"What good is that going to do?"

"Then we give the dress to your friend at Turn the Page, the force of nature."

"Ariela? Where's she going to wear a getup like this?"

"She's not." He leaned back in his chair and smiled. "She's going to auction it off for the charity."

Silence. He was about to concede defeat when she spoke.

"Damn. That is a brilliant idea." She paused and he could almost picture her biting her lip, warring with herself. "But it's a lot of money for you to give away."

"I'll get a tax write-off and I'll be able to sleep with a clear conscience." He dropped his feet from the desk and sat upright. "So, what do you say?"

"I say yes." She paused and for a moment he thought she'd hung up until she spoke again. "And thank you."

14

"FUCKITY FUCK FUCK FUCK." Devin paced self-consciously in front of Lincoln Center's iconic plaza fountain, watching the rich and famous make their way toward the Koch Theater, where the ballet performed. She tightened her grip on the faded pashmina she'd covered her shoulders with despite the sweltering late August heat. Even with her tattoos hidden and three of the four piercings in her ear removed, she felt the stares of the passersby.

You can take the girl out of the Heights, but you can't take the Heights out of the girl.

She stopped pacing and checked to make sure her ink was totally concealed, adjusting the long shawl so it draped behind her, hiding the top of the sugar skull just visible above the low back of her dress. This was a big, fat, freaking mistake. She belonged at a society event as much as a nun belonged in a biker bar.

She was about ten seconds from bolting when a deep, smoky voice came from behind her. "Juliet."

She turned and found Gabe, looking hotter than hot in a well-fitting, single-breasted black tuxedo, crisp white shirt and black bow tie, a red rose extended in one hand. "Romeo, I presume?"

"At your service." He bowed low and handed her the flower.

"Thank you." She brought it to her nose and inhaled,

her eyes on the patrons as they streamed into the theater. Too late to back out now. "I guess we'd better get inside."

He took in her wrap. "It's almost ninety degrees. What's with the granny garb?"

"I, uh, thought it might be cold in the theater." She clutched it closer to her.

He scanned the crowd. "No one else seems concerned. Besides, you'll never make Page Six in that thing."

Devin groaned. He was right. Most of the women flooding past were showing some skin. Only there was a big difference between their unblemished flesh and hers.

"Unless there's some other reason you're clinging to it like it's a life preserver and you're a passenger on the *Titanic*." He put his hands on her upper arms and drew the shawl down to her wrists. "Like you don't want anyone to see your tattoos."

Damn him. How did he do that?

"I don't… I'm not…"

He reached up and fingered her earlobe. "Then why did you take out your piercings?"

"I figured you'd want me to look like everyone else." Or as alike as she could get.

He took the wrap from her unprotesting fingers, balled it up in his fist and stood back to admire her. "Much better. You look beautiful. More than beautiful. Flawless."

"But everyone else here is…"

"Not you." He touched her hair, so lightly she barely felt it, like the gentlest summer breeze. She'd left it hanging loose, a decision she was beginning to regret, surrounded by fancy up-dos in all shapes and sizes. "I invited you. I want to be here with you. Not some sanitized version of who you think you should be."

"You realize these are your constituents, right?" She waved an arm at the crowd on the plaza. "The people who are going to be voting for you. Or against you, if you give them a reason to. Like your *grencha* girlfriend."

She stumbled on the last word, but he didn't seem to notice. A smile crept across his face. "I like the sound of 'girlfriend.' But what's *grencha* mean?"

"Cheap. Trashy." She stuck a hand on her hip and struck the classic hooker pose, almost as if to prove her point. "What most people assume when they see my ink."

"If they're shallow enough to believe that, I don't want their vote." He held out his arm. "Shall we?"

The knot in her stomach loosened. If Gabe wanted her to do this—believed she could do this—then damn it, she would. She nodded, taking his elbow, and he handed back her pashmina before steering her into the swarm of people heading to the theater. She promptly tossed the bargain-basement scarf into a nearby garbage can on their way.

Inside, they barely had time to greet Gabe's family— minus Ivy, who was in Brazil shooting the centerfold for the *Sports Illustrated* swimsuit issue—and sit down before the lights dimmed and the curtain went up.

"What do you think?" he whispered in her ear about ten minutes into the performance, reaching over the armrest to take her hand.

"You sister is wonderful." She linked her fingers with his and squeezed. "They're all wonderful."

"You can tell them so yourself at the after-party."

Tension started to build again inside her, twisting her gut with anxiety. "Right. The after-party."

Which she'd been trying not to think about. She'd actually have to make polite conversation with the folks who'd been giving her the evil eye, her tattoos on full display in glorious Technicolor. People would point and whisper about her behind her back. Or, even worse, to her face.

Tramp.

Slut.

Whore.

Suddenly she understood how Gabe had felt at the rave. Out of his element. Insecure. It wasn't a feeling she liked, or one she wanted to get used to.

"Can't wait." She gave him a forced smile and turned her attention back to the swans and princes pirouetting and jeté-ing across the stage. As magical as it was, she couldn't shake the sense that this night was a disaster waiting to happen.

"What's wrong?" Gabe asked at intermission, plucking two champagne glasses from a passing waiter's tray and handing one to her. "You look like you swallowed a lemon."

"Nothing." She took a slow, fortifying sip of the bubbly liquid. "Just tired, I guess."

A middle-aged woman in a silver sequined gown waved to Gabe from across the room. He nodded in acknowledgment and Devin crossed her fingers behind her back, willing her not to approach them. She breathed a relieved sigh when the woman was waylaid by someone who looked a lot like Sarah Jessica Parker.

Gabe snaked his free arm around her waist. Heat radiated from his hand on the bare skin of her lower back. "If it's the after-party you're worried about, don't be."

Who was this guy? The Long Island Medium?

"I meant what I said outside," he continued, guiding her into a remote corner of the lobby where they could talk as privately as possible with hundreds of people milling around. "I don't want you to be anything but who you are. And if these people can't accept that, that's their problem."

"But the election…"

"We're a package deal, sweetheart. I'm not running my life around a campaign." For a second, a sort of far-away look crossed his face, like his mind had gone somewhere else. Then he shook his head and his eyes cleared. When he spoke, his tone was determined and the hand on her back pulled her closer to him. "Not anymore."

Devin was saved from trying to form a response by Holly, who ran up to squeal over Devin's gown with Nick in tow. The four spent the rest of the break together until the lights flickered and they returned to their seats.

The second act was shorter than the first, and before she knew it Devin was walking the red carpet to the gala on Gabe's arm, stopping and smiling as flashbulbs popped in their faces.

"Having fun?" he murmured between flashes.

"It's a little blinding," she admitted, blinking. "But definitely a once in a lifetime experience."

"Not if I get elected."

Another thought she'd tried to ignore. Odds were she wouldn't have to deal with it. The chances of them still being together then were about the same as a snowball stood in hell.

But what if...

"Gabe. Devin. Over here."

Devin turned to see a tall, lanky man in jeans and a white button-down smiling at them, an expensive-looking camera in one hand.

"This one's for Page Six," he said with a wink, lifting the camera to his face.

"Thanks, Tom. My buddy at the *Post*," Gabe whispered in her ear as they posed. "This is our money shot. Show him your good side."

"All my sides are good," she quipped.

He leaned in closer and lowered his voice to a sexy growl. "Can't argue with you there. I like everything I've seen so far."

"Great job, guys." Tom strode over to them, his camera at his side. "I've got what I need. It'll be in tomorrow's edition."

"Thanks again, man." Gabe shook his hand. "I owe you one."

"Anything for a fair maiden." Tom winked again and pulled out a business card from his shirt pocket. "Here. Email me. I'll send you copies of all your pics for the auction."

She took the card. "Thanks."

"Watch out for this guy," he called, gesturing to Gabe as he blended back into the throng of paparazzi. "He may look harmless, but he's a regular lady-killer."

Don't I know it, she thought, letting Gabe lead her down the red carpet and into the party. He'd just about slayed her.

"DEVIN SEEMS TO be enjoying herself." Nick sidled up to Gabe at the bar.

Gabe didn't have to look to know Nick was right. He'd been at Devin's side most of the evening. She was radiant. A rare, exotic creature in a sea of conformity.

He turned and found her in the center of the room with Holly and the mayor's wife. Her initial unease seemed to have deserted her and she was talking animatedly.

"She sure does," Gabe agreed, his heart overflowing with pride.

She hadn't wanted to admit it, but he knew she was nervous about mingling with the high and mighty. Thought they would judge her on her appearance, and she wasn't altogether wrong. She'd endured her share of stares and whispers from the upper crust, but just as many people had come up and introduced themselves, curious to find out who she was and what she was doing there. Many had stayed to chat, as captivated by her as he was.

Gabe nodded to Nick's empty glass. "Need a refill? I'm buying."

"It's open bar."

"I know."

"Great. I'll get the next round." Nick handed his glass to the bartender. "Vodka tonic. And a club soda."

"I thought you were more of a Scotch drinker." Gabe had bought him a bottle of eighteen-year-old Glenmorangie for his bachelor party.

"I am." Nick stuck a bill in the tip container. "But only the good stuff. Which I doubt they have on hand tonight, no matter how high-class this shindig is."

"How's my sister holding up?" Gabe sipped his Manhattan.

Nick's eyes settled on his wife, who stood with one hand on her stomach and the other on her lower back. A crease wrinkled his forehead. "She's exhausted. No big surprise for a woman who's almost five months pregnant. I offered to take her home, but she insists on staying until Noelle makes her grand entrance."

Gabe checked his watch. "Hopefully the prima donna will be out in a few minutes so you guys can say your congratulations and split."

"She needs to take care of herself. After everything she went through last time…"

Nick trailed off and Gabe saw the worry painted all over his face. Holly had struck gold with this guy. Nick was nothing like her scumbag ex, who had beaten her so badly she'd lost their baby. He loved her and would do anything to make sure she and the child she carried stayed healthy and safe.

Gabe's gaze shifted to Devin. He felt himself smile as he pictured her heavy with his child, her tattooed belly swollen, her skin and eyes aglow with impending motherhood.

He was all in with this woman. Like a house-in-the-burbs-with-a-two-car-garage-and-enough-kids-to-field-their-own-basketball-team in. Now if he could just find a way to get her on board…

"Uh, oh." Nick chuckled.

Gabe blinked and faced his brother-in-law. "What?'"

"I'd know that look anywhere. The glazed eyes. The slack jaw. The general aura of lovesickness." Nick clapped Gabe on the shoulder. "You're a goner, my friend. I wouldn't be surprised if we had another wedding in the family before the year's out."

"Who's getting married?"

Damn. It was like his mother had a sixth sense or something. Any time someone discussed marriage she popped up like a prairie dog. Especially if it involved one of her children. With Holly paired off, successfully this time, she now had her sights set on Gabe.

"No one, Mom." Gabe kissed her cheek.

"I wouldn't be so sure of that." Nick grabbed his drinks from the bar. "Excuse me. My lady awaits."

"So much for the bro code," Gabe muttered to his back.

"You and Devin are serious, then?" A good foot shorter than him, his mother's piercing stare had a way of worming the truth out of him. Hell, he'd learned his best cross-examination moves from her. His law school professors and JAG instructors couldn't even come close.

"Well, I am," he admitted. "She's…"

"Wounded," his mother finished, putting a hand on his forearm. "Tread gently with her, Gabriel. Be patient. She'll come around in time."

"It took me almost two years to woo your mother, here." Gabe's father came up beside his wife and put an arm around her shoulders. "Worth every minute."

Great. What was this, a referendum on his love life?

His father bent to place a soft kiss on his wife's forehead and she giggled, something that should have seemed ridiculous for a fifty-five-year-old woman but didn't.

Gabe's momentary irritation faded as quickly as it had begun. He wanted what his parents had, and if it took him two years—or more—to convince Devin... Well, like his father said, it would be worth every minute.

"Thanks, Pop. I'll keep that in mind." A buzz started at the other end of the room. "Look, there's Noelle. Why don't you go see her? I'll find Devin and join you in a few minutes."

The rest of the party passed in a blur. It was almost two hours before he got Devin alone, in a quiet corner at the back of the room. "What do you say, sweetheart?" He dropped a kiss on her forehead, much like his father had done to his mother earlier. "Ready to go?"

"This whole night is like a fairy tale." She spun in a circle, arms extended, making the bottom of her gown flare out around her ankles. "I don't want it to end."

Her twirling morphed into a wobble, and he reached out to steady her. "The clock's about to strike twelve. And I think this Cinderella's had a little too much to drink."

"Maybe a teensy-weensy bit." She held up her thumb and forefinger, so close they were almost touching.

"Come on, princess." He took her hand, kissed it and tucked it into his arm. "Let's get you home."

"Home?" She pouted up at him. "I don't wanna go home."

He brushed a lock of hair off her cheek. "My home."

"Oh." She brightened. "Well, that's different. I like it there. Your bed's a lot bigger than mine. And softer."

"It certainly is." He pressed his lips together, fighting hard not to laugh. She was damned cute when she was tipsy, if a woman with a spider web peeking out from behind one ear and a skull on her back could be considered cute. And damned horny, too, he thought as she rubbed up against him like a cat in heat.

"You know what else I like?" She rested her head on his

shoulder, and he breathed in her almond shampoo, mixed with a hint of the Chanel No. 5 she favored. "I like you."

"I like you, too." Wrong *L* word, but he'd take what he could get. "Now how about we get out of here before our cab turns into a pumpkin and you lose one of those sexy shoes?"

15

UNDER THE THICK fleece blanket, Devin stretched on the comfortable mattress. Rolling over to her stomach, she settled her face into the fluffy pillow.

Hold the freaking phone. Comfortable mattress? Fluffy pillow? Thick fleece blanket? Where was her fold-out couch with the spring that jabbed her in the side every time she moved? Or the flat-as-a-pancake pillow she'd meant to replace months ago? Or the SpongeBob comforter Holly had given her as a gag gift last Christmas?

She rolled to one side and inched an eye open, adjusting to the darkness of a bedroom that was considerably larger than hers. After a minute, she could make out an armchair in the corner, a glittering red gown over its back. The beading caught the light that streamed through a break in the curtains covering the floor-to-ceiling windows. A pair of matching shoes sat nearby, and a lacy black bra and panties dangled above them from the arm of the chair.

Fucking hell.

The events of the previous night came rushing back. She groaned and buried her face into the pillow again.

Two drinks. That's all she'd had. Not even serious drinks. Silly, fruity things, with cherries and umbrellas. She figured she'd play it safe with the girly stuff. Man, was she wrong. That bartender must have had a heavy pour. He wouldn't last one shift at Naboombu.

She turned her head and her heart jumpstarted at the sight of Gabe, spread-eagled on his back next to her, gloriously naked, his share of the blanket in a heap at his feet. His eyes were closed, his sinfully long lashes dark against his cheeks. An uncharacteristic hint of stubble shadowed his jaw and she longed to reach out and feel it rasp against her palm.

You know what I like? I like you.

Had she actually said that to him?

Jesus Christ.

Oh, well. Water under the Brooklyn Bridge. She couldn't take it back, even if she wanted to. Alcohol might have loosened her lips, but what had come out of them wasn't exactly a lie. She did like Gabe. Maybe more than like him.

And, hell, it could have been worse. He could have laughed in her face. Or—her skin crawled at the thought— she could have slipped and used the other *L* word. Drunk or sober, she'd never said *that* to any man.

Devin groaned again and let her face sink into the pillow.

"Morning, Sleeping Beauty."

She peeked at Gabe with one eye. He rolled to his side to face her, propping his head up on one arm. The start of his morning erection lay dangerously close to her hip.

"What happened to Cinderella?" she asked.

"You tell me."

Devin pulled the blanket over her head. "She got drunk and made an idiot out of herself."

"Not drunk. Tipsy." He inched the blanket down to her shoulders. "And certainly not an idiot."

"All those people…" Her voice trailed off and she threw an arm over her eyes.

"Loved you," he finished for her, drawing her arm down bringing his face so close to hers she had no choice but to meet his gaze. "You were magnificent."

"I doubt that." Her eyes darted to her clothes. "Did we…?"

"No." His face grew serious, his gray eyes earnest. "I'm not in the habit of taking advantage of unsuspecting women."

No, he wouldn't be. Doing it with a tipsy girl wasn't in the Gabe Nelson code of conduct. He'd taken care, not advantage, of her. Put her needs before his.

She licked her lips. "Are you in the habit of letting them take advantage of you?"

"That depends."

"On what?"

He gave her a wolfish smile. "On what you had in mind."

"How about this?"

She threw off the covers and slid down his body, licking a trail from his chest, over the ridges and valleys of his rock-hard abs, to the line of hair that ran from his navel to groin.

"I like the direction you're going." His voice rumbled over her like thunder.

She wrapped her fingers around him and traced the head of his cock with her tongue. "You'll like it even better in about two seconds."

"I like it a whole hell of a lot already."

She pumped him twice with her hand and took him into her mouth. He tasted equal parts sweat and salt and soap. *Delicious.*

"You're right." Gabe arched his back, thrusting into her warm, waiting mouth. "I do like it better."

She relaxed her jaw and took him deeper, swallowing when she felt him bump against the back of her throat.

"Fuck, yeah." He flexed his hips and brought one hand to the back of her head, not aggressively but gently, holding her where he wanted her as he continued to move inside her.

Devin hummed around him and sucked harder, even more turned on by the knowledge that she had the power to make him lose control. She'd never bought into the idea that giving head was an act of submission. How could it be, when she had Gabe exactly where she wanted him? Desperate, panting, vulnerable.

At her mercy.

She flicked her tongue along the underside of his cock and cupped his balls, teasing them with her fingernails as she worked her mouth over him.

"God, Devin," Gabe moaned. "Don't stop. Just like that."

Her free hand snaked down to her pussy so she could stroke herself in time with his thrusts.

"Shit. I'm going to come."

He tried to withdraw but she swallowed him deeper and plunged a finger inside herself, only a heartbeat away from exploding.

"I can't hold back," he pleaded. "If you don't stop…"

She released him long enough to answer, echoing words he'd said to her only days before.

"Please." She raised her eyes to his and was met with a pure, raw hunger she was sure was reflected in her own. "Let me do this for you."

She didn't wait for his response, wrapping her fingers around the base of his cock and sliding her lips over his crown. Her fingers moved furiously over her clit, and she came just as he did, swallowing her cries with his come.

"No fair," he growled as she crawled up his body, exploring with her hands and mouth as she went.

"Seriously?" She settled her head under his chin and curved one leg over his hip, hesitating for a second to wonder when the hell she'd become a cuddler. "You're going to complain after that?"

She felt him smile against her hair. "Only because I didn't get to return the favor."

"I'm sure we can fix that." She drew slow circles around his nipple with her index finger. "Leo's not expecting me at the shop until noon."

"Noon, huh?" He flipped her onto her back and loomed over her, looking like a dark, foreboding angel. "Not nearly enough time for what I'm thinking."

He pressed a kiss to her temple then moved lower, lower, planting kisses like breadcrumbs until he reached the triangle of hair she left unshaven above her sex. "But I guess I'll have to make do."

"ARE YOU GOING to tell me where you're taking me, or not?" Devin eyed Gabe, in the driver's seat next to her, with a raised brow.

"Not." Gabe's eyes never strayed from the traffic crowding FDR Drive.

She rested her head against the car window and crossed her arms. It had been two weeks since he'd sprung the whole dress thing on her. Had the man learned nothing?

"You know," she said, "this could be considered kidnapping."

"As head of the Special Victim's Bureau, I feel safe in saying it's not."

She frowned. "I told you before, I hate surprises."

"Trust me." He merged onto the ramp for the Midtown Tunnel. "You'll like this one. Just like you liked the museum. And the dress, even if it did take some of my best smooth talking to get you to wear it."

He had a point. Gabe's surprises were usually of the welcome variety. Hell, the dress had wound up netting more than it was worth for Turn the Page.

But she still couldn't help feeling anxious. In her pre-Gabe experience, surprises pretty much always sucked. As in surprise, your dad's gone. Or surprise, throw your stuff in a grocery bag, you're moving. Again.

"It must be something big if you got Leo to cut me loose on a Saturday. And hauled your car out of the garage."

"Leo was very accommodating." Gabe slowed for the toll. "And it's too far to take a taxi."

"Kidnapping," she muttered, pulling out her iPod and putting in her earbuds. His classical stuff was okay, but the mood she was in now required something with more of a beat. Something she could do a little headbanging to.

About forty minutes and almost all of the Foo Fighters' *Wasting Light* later, Gabe shook her shoulder. "We there yet?" she asked, taking out one earbud.

"Almost." He maneuvered the car off the exit.

She looked out the window. Trees. Grass. Suburban sprawl. They definitely weren't in Kansas anymore. "Where are we?"

"Long Island." He turned onto a treelined side street. "Huntington."

"What's way out here?"

"You'll see. Be patient."

"Not one of my strong suits."

"So I've noticed." He took his eyes off the road just long enough to shoot her a smartass grin. "But this will be worth the wait. I promise."

She stowed her iPod in her purse and stared at the neighborhoods whizzing past the window. Freaking McMansions, with perfectly manicured lawns, sculptured gardens and elaborate playscapes.

Exactly the kind of home she'd dreamed of having as a kid.

"Picture perfect," she muttered. He turned down another street and the houses gradually got smaller, quaint Capes with tidy lawns, unremarkable landscaping and swing sets you could find at Target.

What she would have given for any one of them...

"I've never actually been to Long Island." It was safer revealing that tidbit than reopening her childhood wounds. "If you want to get technical, aside from our little jaunt to Connecticut to see Holly, I've never been outside the five boroughs."

"Really?"

"Really. If the subway doesn't go there, I don't go."

"We'll have to do something about that. Start small. Maybe a weekend in Vermont next month. My old navy commander has a cabin there we're welcome to use."

A weekend? In Vermont? Going away together meant they were getting serious, didn't it? And she didn't do serious. Admitting she had feelings for him was one thing. But taking things to the next level? Throwing around words like *commitment* and *forever*?

No fucking way. No fucking how.

Devin wrapped her arms around herself, her stomach rolling with fresh nerves. If Gabe was thinking about shit like weekend getaways and lifetime commitment, who knew what was waiting for her at the end of this car ride?

"We're here." He pulled to the curb in front of a split-level ranch, shut off the engine and turned to her. "You're off the hook. For now. But don't think we won't revisit this after..."

He paused and swallowed, making his Adam's apple dance in his throat.

"After what?" She reached for the door handle, stopping short at the sight of a psychedelic orange and green minivan in the driveway. "Who lives here? The Partridge Family? Scooby-Doo and the gang?"

"Follow me and find out."

He led her up the flagstone walkway and paused at the front door, his finger hovering over the doorbell.

"What are you waiting for?" She balled her hands into fists on her hips. "You're freaking me out."

"Sorry." He pressed the button and a musical chime sounded from inside. With his other hand, he gave her shoulder a squeeze that was probably meant to be reassuring but did little to calm her jangling nerves. "That's the last thing I want to do."

"Then tell me…"

Before she could finish, a woman about Devin's age in navy blue sweats with a logo over her left breast that read Haven House opened the door. "Gabe, it's good to see you again. And you must be Devin. We've been expecting you."

"Again?" Devin shot a glance at Gabe. He responded with a shrug. "And who's we?"

"The boys have been a handful this morning. We don't see many new faces around here." The woman stood back and held the door open so they could enter.

Boys? What was this place, some sort of glorified frat house?

"Yeah," a man who looked to be in his early twenties, dressed in identical blue sweats, piped up from behind the woman. "Especially ones as pretty as yours."

And what was with the matching outfits?

Gabe put a protective—or was it possessive?—arm around Devin's waist.

"Down, Pete." The woman gave him a teasing poke in the ribs. "Can you take Devin and her friend to the screen porch?"

She turned back to Devin. "Victor is waiting for you there."

"Sure." The man waved his arm for them to follow him and started up the stairs to the main floor. "Come on."

But Devin stood rooted to the faux marble tile in the entryway, unable to move. Tears pooled in her eyes as she looked up at Gabe.

"You found him?"

Gabe nodded.

"You're sure?" She held on to the strap of her purse like it was the safety bar on a roller coaster, capable of keeping her from tumbling through space and winding up in a crumpled heap on the ground. "It's really him?"

She'd run down so many false leads. Had so many close calls, only to end up disappointed. What if this was just one more?

"It's him. Murphy—my inspector—tracked down Victor's last set of foster parents. They remembered that the couple who adopted him was from Oyster Bay. It wasn't hard to trace him from there."

"Excuse me," the woman said. "Why don't you both come upstairs to the living room? You can talk privately there. Pete will take you to Victor when you're ready."

Gabe looked questioningly at Devin and she nodded, swiping away tears with her forearm. They followed the woman up the steps to a large, sunlit room with a worn but clean couch, two overstuffed chairs and a TV.

"Make yourselves at home," she said, already heading down a long hall that Devin assumed led to the bedrooms. "I'll tell Pete to give you a few minutes."

Devin sank into one of the chairs. "So this place is…"

"A group home for autistic adults," Gabe finished, sitting across from her on the couch.

"What about Victor's adoptive parents?"

Gabe shook his head. "Dead. But they were fairly well off. Set up a trust fund for him to make sure he was taken care of after they were gone."

Devin closed her eyes and sagged back. She'd had so many questions for them, the chief one being did they know she existed? And if so, did they try to find her? Or let her rot in foster care without a second thought?

Then again, maybe she didn't want answers. Maybe ignorance really was bliss, or at least less painful.

"So he's got no one," she said. "Like me."

"Not anymore." Gabe's voice was low, almost a whisper.

Her eyes flew open. "What if he doesn't remember me?"

"Here." Gabe pulled a tattered stuffed animal out of a bag she hadn't even realized he'd been holding. "This might help."

"Tex." She blinked. "How did you get this? It was in the drawer next to my bed."

"Remember that night we thought we ran out of condoms?" A devilish grin stretched across his face.

Oh, yeah. She remembered, all right. He'd taken to stopping by Naboombu when she was working. Then, when her shift was over, they'd go back to her place and do their best to single-handedly keep whoever manufactured Trojans in business. On the night in question, they'd found the box she kept in her lingerie drawer empty. They'd made a game of ransacking her apartment for spare condoms, in between kisses and cuddles.

"I saw it then," he continued, snapping her back to the present. "I smuggled it out in my briefcase yesterday morning when you were in the shower."

He held the toy out and she took it, cradling the animal's faded body to her chest.

"Thank you." The words seemed so small, so inadequate. But she didn't have any others.

Pete cleared his throat in the doorway. "Ready to see your brother?"

Devin wiped her moist hands on her skinny jeans and stood. "As I'll ever be."

"He's good today. Talking, making eye contact." Pete raised a shoulder. "But I don't know how long it'll last."

"Yeah." She let out a slow sigh, remembering the good days, when Victor made the bus on time, got glowing reports from his teachers and even helped get dinner on the table. And the bad ones, when he'd refuse to get dressed, dump his cereal on the floor and scream and lash out at everything in his path. When nothing Devin did could reach past the invisible wall around him. "I get that."

She began to follow Pete before she realized Gabe wasn't behind her. She turned to find Gabe still sitting on the couch, his Sperry-clad foot resting on one knee. "Aren't you coming with me?"

"No. This is your time with your brother." He got up and walked over to her, enfolding her in his strong arms.

"But don't worry." He spoke into her hair, his lips grazing her scalp. "I'll be right here waiting for you when you're done. No matter how long it takes."

He gave her a gentle push and she followed Pete down the hall to a screened-in porch at the back of the house.

"Here we are." Pete stopped at the doorway. "Just holler if you need anything. I'll be right here."

"Thanks."

Devin took a deep breath and stepped inside. The room was sunny and warm, with comfy, cushioned wicker chairs scattered around. In one of them sat Victor, his head bent over a hand-held computer game.

Even if Devin hadn't known he'd be waiting for her there, she'd have recognized him immediately. The mop of unruly, dark curls. The scar on his left cheek from when she'd tried to teach him to ride a bike. The way he bit his bottom lip in concentration, just like he had as a kid.

She brushed away a tear and pulled up a chair next to him, close but not so close that she'd startle him.

"Hey, buddy." She held out Tex. "I brought something for you."

He didn't lift his head.

"Look." She tried again, putting the stuffed animal on his lap. "It's Tex. Remember him?"

"Tex." Victor let the computer game fall to his side and reached out a hand to pet the armadillo. "My Tex."

"That's right." Her voice was thick with emotion. "Your Tex. And I'm your sister, Devin."

He clutched the stuffed animal to his chest and looked up at her, his coal-black eyes filled with the same wonder he'd had as a child. "Devin?"

She nodded, unable to speak.

"Devin always bought me Push Ups from the ice cream truck."

She swallowed a happy sob, remembering how she'd squirrel away change from the couch cushions to make sure Victor could have his favorite treat at least once a week in the summer. He remembered, too. "I sure did."

"Can you get me one now?" He bounced in his seat.

Paul, who had obviously been listening on the other side of the doorway, popped his head in. "I don't know about a Push Up. But we've got some rocky road in the freezer. How about I bring you a bowl?"

"What do you say, Victor?" Devin put a tentative hand on her brother's knee. She said a silent prayer of thanks when he let it stay there.

"Okay." His eyes met hers for an instant. "But you have to have some, too."

"Sure, buddy." She nodded, blinking back tears. "I'd like that."

16

"You win." Gabe laid his cue across the table. "Again."

"Third scratch in a row." Cade clucked his tongue. "Dude, you suck tonight. And your mood's not much better. What crawled up your butt and died?"

"Do you want to play another round or not?" Gabe started to rack up the balls.

"Not. And you didn't drive all the way up to Stockton just for me to school you at pool. Or to drink the Half Pint's watered-down beer." Cade hung his cue up in the rack on the wall next to the jukebox that hadn't worked since disco was king of the charts. "What gives?"

"Can't a guy want to spend some time with his best friend?"

"Not when he's got a smoking hot woman waiting for him back in the city." Cade leaned on the jukebox. "Unless you screwed that up already."

"I did not screw it up." Gabe left the balls where they were and hung his cue next to Cade's. "I'm giving Devin some space. She's been spending a lot of time with her brother the past couple of weeks. Reconnecting with him."

"Space my ass." Cade slung an arm around Gabe's shoulders and commandeered him toward the bar. "You're preparing yourself for the fall."

"The what?"

"The fall. The letdown. The end."

Gabe dropped onto a stool and rested his elbows on the bar. "End of what?"

"Of whatever it is you're doing with Elvira Mistress of the Dark." Cade pulled out the stool beside him and sat.

Smacking his so-called friend in the arm, Gabe motioned for the bartender. "I told you to stop calling her that."

Cade didn't budge. "Face it, bro. She got what she wanted. Her brother. And now you're afraid she's going to cut and run."

"Whatever, Dr. Phil."

"Hey, Cade." The pretty female bartender leaned over the rail, giving them an eyeful of what looked like the world's biggest man-made breasts spilling out of her low-cut top. She flashed Cade a thousand-watt smile. "Long time no see."

He shrugged. "I've been busy."

Her smile dimmed for a split second before she recovered and ran a hand through her long, equally manufactured, bleach-blond hair. "What'll it be?"

"Bud for me and a…" He eyeballed Gabe.

"Black & Tan," Gabe finished.

"Black & Tan for my lovesick friend." Cade pulled a twenty out of his wallet and slid it across the bar.

Gabe slapped his hand down on the bill before the bartender could grab it. "I'm not lovesick. And this round's on me."

"No way." Cade shook his head. "My hangout. My money."

"If I let you pay, will you stop psychoanalyzing me?"

"Fat chance." Cade chuckled. "I'm just getting started."

The bartender rolled her baby blues at them. "You guys can figure this out while I get your drinks."

She moved off to the other end of the bar.

"Fine." Gabe pushed the twenty at his friend. "Then you're paying for the next round, too."

Cade smiled and lifted an invisible glass in a mock toast. "Let the analysis begin."

"I've got a better idea. How about we discuss what's with you and the bartender?"

"Simple. She's interested. I'm not."

Gabe choked back a laugh. "Blonde. Blue eyes. Big boobs. I would've thought she was just your type."

A shadow of something Gabe couldn't quite identify crossed Cade's face. "Maybe my type's changed."

"Yeah. And maybe Jimmy Hoffa's alive and well and living in a tent in my parents' backyard."

"Here you go, boys." The bartender plunked two foamy mugs down in front of them and batted her eyes at Cade. "Let me know if you need anything else."

"I'll bet," Cade muttered, taking a sip of his beer as she sauntered away. He eyed Gabe over his mug. "Now you. Fess up."

"There's nothing to fess. Devin and I are hanging out. That's it."

"So you're friends with benefits? Is that what you're saying?" Cade took another slug of beer and wiped his mouth on his sleeve. "Because that's always been more my scene than yours."

"Not my choice."

"Man, oh, man. This chick has you tied up in knots."

"You can say that again."

"So what are you going to do about it?"

"Do?" Gabe gulped his Black & Tan, needing something to take his mind of the ridiculous conversation they were having. "Nothing."

"When did you become such a pussy?"

"I am not a pussy."

"What else do you call someone who's afraid to man

up and tell the woman he loves how he feels about her?" Cade asked.

Gabe almost spat beer at him. "Who said anything about love?"

"You did." Cade gestured toward the mirror on the other side of the bar. "See for yourself. The hangdog expression. The dark circles under your eyes. Your even more sour than usual disposition."

"Shit."

Was he that obvious? Apparently.

Cade drummed his fingers on the bar rail. "I repeat, what are you going to do about it, Casanova?"

"What can I do?" Gabe asked. "If I—as you so eloquently put it—man up, she'll freak."

"You don't know that."

"She's not exactly in the market for a long-term relationship. She's been burned one too many times before."

"Give her a chance. Until you do, you're living in limbo, waiting for the other shoe to drop." Cade swiveled on his stool to face Gabe. "Which is worse, knowing or not knowing?"

Gabe grimaced and looked away, pretending to watch whatever game was playing on the flat-screen at the end of the bar. As much as he didn't want to admit it, the guy had a point. "I thought you didn't like Devin."

"I don't. For me. But for you..." Cade paused. When he started speaking again, all hints of joking were gone. "Weirdly enough, I can see you guys together. She's your other half. The yin to your yang. The Beyoncé to your Jay-Z."

Gabe turned back to his friend. "Pretty strong words from a confirmed bachelor."

"Who said I was a confirmed bachelor?" Cade pushed his empty mug across the bar and signaled for a refill. "I just haven't met the right one yet. You have. Anyway, she's a damn sight better than that ice princess you almost married."

Jesus Christ. How was it everyone else had seen through Kara before he did? Thank God she'd turned him down. Otherwise he might never have known what it was really like to have your ass handed to you on a platter by love.

"So what do you say?" Cade prodded him. "Are you going to step up to the plate and go for it?"

"Yeah. I am." Gabe downed the rest of his Black & Tan and set his empty mug down next to Cade's. "But I'm warning you. You better be ready to buy me another twenty rounds if it all goes to shit."

"I'm in. As long as there's no crying." Cade pushed back his stool and stood. "Enough male bonding. Come on. It's time for me to school you in darts, too."

GABE STEPPED UP to a table under a sign that read Nonni Zaneta's Fried Dough.

"Two *zeppole*," he said, using the traditional word his mother had taught him for the deep-fried treat. "Extra sauce."

"Just powdered sugar on mine," Devin corrected.

"Powdered sugar?" Gabe teased. "What kind of Italian are you?"

"The Hispanic kind."

"Look around." He gestured at the street, packed with people of all shapes and sizes, many dressed in the red, white and green of the Italian flag and gorging themselves on sausage and peppers, pizza and cannoli. "It's the Feast of San Gennaro. Today, everyone's Italian."

She looked wistful. "I wish Victor could have come. He loves fried dough. But all these sights and sounds and smells would have overwhelmed him."

"Maybe next year. And we can bring him some *zeppole* the next time we visit."

"He'd like that." She tapped a loose fist to her chest, making Gabe feel like a superhero for a simple suggestion.

Trying to keep his emotions in check, he reached in his pants pocket for a twenty to pay the vendor. His fingers brushed against the key he'd had made that morning and put on a ring with the Matisse family crest and the slogan "Keep Calm and Paint."

He wasn't stupid enough to get down on one knee and propose to Devin at the festival. Way too soon for that. But he wanted her to know that he was all in, one hundred percent, for the duration. And giving her her own key to his apartment would send that message loud and clear.

"Nelson." Thaddeus Holcomb's voice cut through the crowd like a hot knife through mozzarella. "There you are."

Gabe handed Devin her sugared dough and put a hand on her back.

"Mr. Holcomb." With one hand on Devin and the other laden with *zeppole*, Gabe could only nod at his boss. "I thought we weren't meeting until one."

"Got here a little early. Looks like we had the same idea." He waved toward Nonni Zaneta's. "Sustenance before schmoozing."

Holcomb turned his attention to Devin. "And who's this lovely lady?"

Gabe slid his hand around her waist. "I'd like you to meet my girlfriend, Devin."

She stiffened at *girlfriend*. In truth, he didn't like the word any more than she did. It made them sound like goddamned teenagers. But it would have to do, until he could convince her to take on another title. Like fiancée. Or wife.

"It's a pleasure." Holcomb's eyes flitted up and down Devin's frame, no doubt taking in the way her skirt hugged her thighs and her V-neck top dipped just low enough to show a hint of smooth, round cleavage, emblazoned with the bright reds, oranges and yellows on the crest of her phoenix tattoo. "I can see why you've been hiding her."

Devin tensed again. Gabe smoothed the cotton of her blouse in what he hoped was a calming gesture. He grinned when she relaxed against him.

"So today's the big day, eh? Think you're ready to greet the populace?"

Holcomb unbuttoned his suit jacket and Gabe bit back a smile. The guy never went anywhere without a coat and tie. Gabe had briefly considered donning one of his custom Armanis, but Devin had convinced him he'd be professional but more relatable in khakis and a polo shirt.

"Yes, sir, I…"

"Oh, he's ready, all right," Devin interrupted. "I hope you've drafted your press release endorsing him."

Holcomb frowned. "She knows about our arrangement?"

"Of course." Gabe barely restrained himself from breaking into a victory dance right there in front of his boss and everyone else at the damned festival. Devin might not want to admit she loved him, but the fact that she'd leaped to his defense spoke volumes. "We don't have any secrets."

"Touching." Holcomb nodded, an amused expression on his face. "And idealistic."

"What's that supposed to mean?" Devin asked, licking powdered sugar from her lip. Gabe thought he saw Holcomb clench his hands for a split second before releasing them.

"You'll find out soon enough," Holcomb said. "The campaign trail can test even the strongest relationship. Speaking of which…"

He held his hand out to a middle-aged woman striding briskly toward him in a crisp, white pantsuit, her hair pulled back into a neat bun. "Here's my beautiful wife."

"There you are." She took her husband's hand, bestowing him with a bright smile before fixing her eyes on Gabe.

"You must be Gabe. I've heard so much about you," she said, her voice polite but measured, like every word was calculated. The perfect political wife, a carbon copy of Kara in twenty years. "All good, of course."

He looked at Devin in her sexy-as-hell, so-not-corporate-America clothes, her ink proudly displayed, chowing down on fried dough, then back to Holcomb's wife, standing rigidly, one hand extended for him to shake. For what seemed like the millionth time he said a silent prayer of thanks he'd dodged that bullet. Sure, he wanted to be district attorney and kick Jack's ass to the curb in the process. But not enough to change who he was. Or who he loved.

"Nice to meet you, too." Gabe shook her hand. Before he could introduce Devin, Holcomb gave his wife a gentle push.

"What do you say we let the ladies explore on their own while we press the flesh. No need to bore them with politics."

Now it was Gabe's turn to tense up. How was he supposed to do this without her?

"You'll be fine." Devin stood on tiptoe to whisper in his ear. "Just like at the pub crawl. And the ballet."

"I had you with me then," he muttered, low enough that Holcomb wouldn't be able to hear him.

"And I'm with you today. Metaphysically speaking, that is." She planted a quick kiss on his cheek and dropped to her heels.

"What about you?" he asked.

"I'll be fine, too." She nudged him toward his boss. "Go. Mingle. Just remember, good communication is more about listening than talking. People want to know you care about what they have to say. And if that doesn't work, picture them in their underwear."

"She's right. Except for the underwear part. That never works." Holcomb checked his watch. "We'll meet back here at four. That should give us plenty of time to greet the masses."

Devin gave him a cheery wave as his boss's wife led her down the street.

Holcomb threw an arm around Gabe's shoulder and steered him in the opposite direction. "Don't worry, my boy. You're in good hands. And so is your young lady."

Right, Gabe thought. *Just what I'm afraid of.*

17

THE MINUTE SHE was sure the men were out of sight, Devin let her smile falter and her shoulders drop.

Damn. Keeping up appearances was tough. Now she understood why movie stars lost it on the paparazzi.

"Exhausting, isn't it?" The older woman put a sympathetic hand on Devin's forearm.

"You can say that again."

"How about we find somewhere we can sit and talk?"

Great. Just what Devin wanted. A cozy chat with her boyfriend's boss's wife. She ignored the way her insides churned at the word *boyfriend* and pasted her phony smile back on, praying it looked authentic. "Sounds good."

They fought their way through the crowd for a few blocks until they spotted a restaurant across the street with available sidewalk seating. A short wait later, a hostess showed them to a table under a red-and-white-striped awning and handed them two menus.

"What do you say to cappuccino and tiramisu?" Mrs. Holcomb closed her menu and laid it on the table. "My treat."

Devin wet her suddenly dry lips. "You don't have to do that."

"I know. I want to."

"Thank you, Mrs. Holcomb." Devin put her menu on top of the older woman's.

"Please. Call me Louise. No need for formalities between fellow political wives."

Devin jerked back so hard she almost knocked over the table. She reached out a hand to steady it. "Oh, Gabe and I aren't married."

"Not yet." Louise's smile reached her twinkling, honey-brown eyes. "But I saw the way he looked at you. That boy didn't want to leave your side. It's only a matter of time before he pops the question."

No, no, no, no, no. She had to be wrong. They'd been clear from the start that whatever they were doing, it was all fun and games, nothing serious and definitely nothing leading to the altar. Hadn't they?

"And from the way you looked at him, I'm fairly certain what your answer will be."

A waiter came, took their order and spirited their menus away. Devin smoothed down her skirt, which had the added benefit of allowing her to wipe her sweaty palms. "We've only been dating a few weeks."

"Sometimes that's all it takes. I knew Teddy was the man for me after our first date."

"Must have been some date," Devin mumbled.

Louise chuckled. "He took me bowling. I beat his pants off. Twenty-seven years of marriage, and he still won't admit he let me win."

Twenty-seven years? Devin didn't think she knew anyone married that long, except maybe Gabe's parents. In her world, the average life expectancy of a marriage was measured in single digits.

"So." Louise sat back in her chair and folded her hands in her lap. "Is there anything you'd like to ask me?"

"About what?"

"About life in the political spotlight."

"Spotlight?"

"You have no idea what you're in for, do you?" Louise paused for the waiter, who had returned with their drinks and desserts. He set them down and she dismissed him with a nod and a quick but warm "thank you" before continuing. "During the campaign, you'll be living under a microscope. Every word you say, every move you make, will be dissected and analyzed in the court of public opinion."

Devin nibbled at her tiramisu, not sure how to respond.

"Then, if Gabe is elected, he'll be the face of the criminal-justice system for the entire city. And so will you, by extension."

"What are you trying to tell me?" Devin let her fork fall to her plate with a clang. "That I can't hack it?"

Louise smiled indulgently and sipped her cappuccino. "To the contrary. You strike me as a young woman who can handle just about anything. But you should know exactly what you'll be up against."

"And what is that?"

"The press will pick you apart. Your clothes, your hair, your lifestyle. And it's your job to smile, nod and look pretty. You can't respond, can't defend yourself. It can be frustrating, maddening even. But worth it, if you love him." Louise cut off a tiny corner of her tiramisu and lifted it to her mouth. "And I can tell you do."

There she goes again. How could this woman know with such certainty what Devin herself was so unsure of?

Devin started to deny it for a second time, but Louise cut her off with a wave of her fork.

"Never mind me. I've scared you, and that wasn't my intention. Let's enjoy our dessert. Tell me about your artwork." She gestured at the nymph on Devin's shoulder. "I've always wanted to get a tattoo. Something discreet, maybe on my ankle or my hip. Does it hurt much?"

They passed the rest of the meal talking about more comfortable topics, like music and art and the annoying habit men had of not putting the cap back on the tooth-paste. When they were done eating, they walked the fair, stopping occasionally to look at the displays. Devin was surprised to find that Louise was recognized a few times in her own right.

"For my charity work," she explained after talking with one particularly enthusiastic fan. "One of the few benefits of notoriety. You can use your fame to bring attention to causes you believe in. It'll also get you prime seating at Estela."

For a moment Devin pictured herself handing one of those ridiculous, oversize checks to Ariela for Turn the Page. Then she brought herself up short. What the hell was she thinking? There wasn't any future for her and Gabe. And there wasn't going to be any money for Turn the Page, either.

Louise stopped in front of a souvenir stand packed with everything from Italian cookbooks and postcards to religious figurines. She pulled her cell phone out of her purse and checked the time. "It's almost four. I think we've given the boys enough time."

She headed off down Mulberry Street with Devin at her heels. Man, the woman could move, even in four-inch pumps. And after hours at the festival, eating, drinking and rubbing elbows with the crowd, her white suit remained as pristine as it was when Devin had first seen her.

Devin looked down at her own outfit. Her favorite Docs—pink, with vintage daisies—looked like someone had stepped all over them wearing steel-toed work boots. Her blouse had slipped dangerously low on one boob and her skirt had a coffee stain the size of Long Island Sound.

In short, she was a hot mess. Definitely not power-wife material.

"Where are we going?" she asked, trying to adjust her

shirt and keep up with Louise at the same time. "The festival goes on for blocks. They could be anywhere."

"If I know my husband—and I do—I know exactly where they are."

Devin followed her to the corner of Grand and Mott, where festival organizers had set up a makeshift stage. Clusters of people stood listening to three tenors singing "O Sole Mio."

"There they are." Louise pointed to a group at one corner of the stage, and Devin could pick out Gabe's close-cropped, dark head above the rest.

"Just as I suspected," Louise said, picking up the pace. "Teddy's a sucker for Italian music. You'd never know his family dates back to the *Mayflower*. And look, Senator and Mrs. Humphries are with them. Wonderful. I haven't seen them in ages."

A distinguished-looking older couple stood with Gabe's boss. As she got closer, Devin saw they weren't alone. A younger version of Louise was chatting with Gabe a short distance away, one hand clinched possessively on his forearm, her perfectly styled blond bob swinging as she laughed at something he said.

Kara.

Devin lagged behind Louise, who continued at full speed toward the group. After a few paces, she stopped to observe the drama. It was like watching a silent movie. The older gentleman—Senator Humphries—motioning for Gabe and his daughter to join them. Laughing, pumping Gabe's arm, congratulating him for something or another. Gabe's boss joining in, patting Gabe on the back, shaking his hand. The women, smiling, nodding, standing by silently and looking pretty, just like Louise described.

The tenors launched into "Volare" and someone jostled Devin from behind. She started moving again, slowly but steadily.

"I knew I'd find you here." Louise sidled gracefully up to her husband, slipping an arm around his waist. "We're a little early. I hope you don't mind."

"Not at all." He bussed her cheek then turned to address the others. "I think I see the governor on the other side of the stage. Please excuse us for a few moments."

He guided his wife through the crowd.

"So." Devin stood awkwardly next to Gabe, not sure what to do with her hands. She settled for clasping them behind her back. "Nice to see you again, Kara."

"Darcy." Kara strengthened her grip on Gabe's arm and shifted closer to him. "Or is it Diana? I'm terrible with names."

"Not the best quality in a socialite." Devin pressed her lips together, trying her hardest not to smirk.

Gabe deftly removed himself from Kara's grasp and draped his arm over Devin's shoulders. "Senator and Mrs. Humphries, this is Devin Padilla. My girlfriend."

"Girlfriend?" The senator frowned. His wife looked up at him, her eyes questioning.

"Yes, Dad. Remember?" Kara shook her head at him. "I told you I met Gabe's new flame at that pub thing for Turn the Page."

Mrs. Humphries looked from her daughter to Gabe and back again. "But I thought... You two are so perfect together. We assumed you'd get past this little spat and make up."

Devin almost swallowed her tongue. "I'd hardly call turning down a proposal a 'little spat.'"

"Proposal?" Mrs. Humphries stared open-mouthed at Kara. "You never said anything about a proposal."

Kara at least had the grace to look embarrassed. "I knew you wouldn't understand."

"I'm sorry if you got the wrong idea, Mrs. Humphries.

Senator. But I'm with Devin now." Gabe's arm around her shoulders tightened. "And that's not going to change."

The senator's scowl deepened. "I'm sure you know this means I can't support you in the election."

"Because he's not dating your daughter?" Devin balled her hands into fists. "Or because he's dating me?"

"Both." Senator Humphries's answer was quick and certain as he studied Devin, his gaze lingering on her tattoos and piercings. "I wouldn't do anything that might make Kara uncomfortable. And I have serious doubts about your suitability as a political partner."

"I disagree," Gabe said before she could respond. "I think Devin will be a tremendous asset. She understands people and knows how to relate to them."

"I'm afraid the power brokers in this town won't see it that way. And without them, you don't stand a chance of winning." With a dismissive wave, he turned to his wife and daughter. "Time to move on, ladies. The governor awaits."

He led his family away.

"Enough business for one day." Gabe steered Devin in the opposite direction. "I'm starving. Want to split a calzone?"

"Sure," Devin agreed even as her insides churned. The senator's criticism kept running through her brain, sprinkled with snippets of Louise's advice. Louise had been wrong about almost everything, but she'd gotten one thing right.

Devin loved Gabe. A bone-crushing, soul-deep love that she'd never felt before and probably wouldn't again. But she couldn't handle the intense scrutiny of the campaign trail, or the guilt she'd feel if she cost him his dream. She'd drag him down, with her tats and piercings, her too-tight clothes and her big, fat mouth. He needed someone poised and polished and practically perfect in every way. A political Mary Poppins. He needed someone like Kara.

There was only one thing to do. She had to break it off with him. Tonight.

"YOU'RE AWFULLY QUIET." Gabe cleared their plates from the table and dumped them in the sink. He'd deal with the dirty dishes later. Hours later, hopefully, after he'd given her the key and they'd migrated to his bedroom, where they could take their time exploring each other's bodies. They'd probably be there already if it wasn't for his ex and her family. "We're supposed to be celebrating."

"Celebrating what?" Devin swirled her glass of cabernet, staring into the purple liquid as if it had hypnotized her. "You heard what the senator said. He's not going to support you after you broke his little girl's heart."

"I did not break his little girl's heart. And for the record, she didn't break mine, either." He wiped his hands on a dishtowel and leaned against the kitchen counter. "Besides, Senator Humphries isn't the only shark in the political ocean."

"I hope so, for your sake."

"You're not still worried about what he said, are you? He's dead wrong. You're fresh, honest. The voters are going to love you."

"So you've told me. But Gabe…"

"No buts." Gabe came over to the table and straddled a chair, folding his arms across the high back. "My boss is endorsing me, thanks to you. That's cause for celebration. And others will, too. So stop worrying."

She put her glass down and slowly raised her head to meet his gaze. "We need to talk."

The four worst words in the English language.

"Me first," he said, his heart pounding so hard he wouldn't be surprised if it could be heard all the way across the Hudson River in New Jersey. He fingered the key still in his pocket, reaching for her with his free hand. "There's something I've wanted to say to you all day."

"Stop. Please." She jumped up, almost tipping over her chair in the process. "I can't do this."

"Do what?" His brows knotted.

"Whatever it is you're going to ask me to do."

"How do you know I'm going to ask you to do anything?"

"You get this look in your eyes. They go all dark and broody, like you've got some sort of diabolical plan." She shook her head. "But that's not the point. The point is, I can't do this anymore, Gabe. I can't be with you."

The *trofie al pesto* he'd made for dinner rolled in his stomach. "What do you mean you can't be with me? Why?"

"I just…can't."

"That's not an answer. If this is about one idiot senator's misguided opinion…"

"It's not." She wiped a hand across her face. "Look, we had fun, right? But we both knew it couldn't last."

"I'll tell you what I know." He shot to his feet and took her hands in his before she could protest. He raised them to his chest and held them there so she could feel the rapid beating of his heart. "I know we're good together. I know you bring out a side of me I never knew existed, one that's more relaxed, happier. I know I want your face to be the last thing I see every night and the first thing I see every morning."

She broke away from him with a bitter laugh. "Like The Rolling Stones say, you can't always get what you want."

"So that's it?" He stuffed his hands in his pockets. The key scraped against his knuckles, taunting him. "That's all the explanation I'm going to get?"

"I'm sorry." She wrapped her arms around herself, rocking back and forth on her heels. "So sorry. I…care for you. Really, I do. And I'll never forget how you found Victor for me…"

Cade's words echoed in his head. *Face it, bro. She got what she wanted. And now you're afraid she's going to cut and run.*

"Right. Our bargain. You've got your brother. I've got my endorsement. Time to go our separate ways."

"Right," she echoed, dropping her arms. He could have sworn he saw tears before she ducked her head, hiding her face in a curtain of dark hair. "Our bargain."

He followed her to the living room. She grabbed her purse from the couch where, not even an hour ago, they'd been making out like a couple of sex-crazed teens. If he had known that was the last time he'd touch her, kiss her… Hell, he would have kept going and never let her up for air until she was willing to admit they belonged together.

"You're a great guy, Gabe." She hitched her purse up on her shoulder and headed for the door. "And you're going to make a great district attorney."

"If I'm so great then why are you leaving?"

She stopped, her hand on the doorknob, but didn't turn. "Like you said, we had a deal. Now it's done. Nothing to keep me here."

"Nothing?" He came up behind her and brushed back the swath of hair over one ear to plant a kiss on her spiderweb tattoo.

"Stop it." She shook him off but not before he felt her tremble. "You're not playing fair."

"All's fair in love and war."

"So you've said before." She yanked the door open. "But this isn't war. And it's not…it's not love, either."

The door slammed behind her, reverberating throughout the apartment.

Gabe sank onto the sofa and reached into his pocket for the key. His instinct was to chuck it across the damned room, but he held himself in check and laid it carefully on the coffee table. He stared at it for a good ten minutes, wondering how the hell everything had gone to shit so fast.

Fuck. Could that have been any worse? Sure, she could have told him he was boring, too. Although at least then he'd understand what went wrong. Instead, she'd given him some bullshit excuse.

He pulled out his cell phone and called Cade.

"Hardesty." Cade's sleep-muffled voice came over the line.

"You on duty?"

"Mmm-hmm." Gabe heard what sounded like sheets rustling in the background. "Night shift. Sleeping at the station."

"Remember that promise you made to buy me twenty rounds when Devin dumped my ass?"

"Yeah."

"Well, it's go time. My place. As soon as you're off." Gabe eyed his almost empty liquor cabinet across the room. "And bring the hard stuff."

18

QUARTER AFTER TEN, and The Mark was practically deserted. Devin hated pulling midweek shifts. Half the time the money wasn't worth the effort. But when her bartender buddy had called and asked her to fill in for him again, she'd jumped on it. Hell, anything was better than sitting at home, pining over Gabe. Even spending the evening in the same room as Fast Fingers Freddie.

"Last one, cowboy." She plunked his mug of cheap-ass, pisswater domestic beer down in front of him. "After this, you're cut off. And I'm calling you a cab."

"Aww, c'mon." He picked it up, sloshing foam on the mahogany bar top. "Couldn't you let me sleep it off here? Or maybe at your place?"

"Have you forgotten how my knee felt in your balls?" She grabbed a clean cloth from under the counter and wiped up the spill. "Because I'm happy to remind you."

He shrugged and gulped his beer. "You can't blame a guy for trying."

"Actually, yes, I can."

She threw the now sopping towel into the sink and reached for the remote for the TV over the bar. The Yanks were way ahead. With no one but Freddie and a couple of off-duty cops who weren't paying attention to the TV, she could find something more entertaining on. Maybe *Chopped*. Or a rerun of *Full House*. She flicked through the channels, stopping when she heard a low-pitched, earnest, clearly recognizable voice.

"Jack Kentfield wants you to believe the city's in a state of crisis. He wants you to believe there are predators lurking around every corner that only he can save you from. Well, the numbers don't lie. And the numbers say violent crime has dropped every year since 1990. Murders are down more than twenty-five percent in the past two years, sexual assaults down almost seven percent and robberies eighteen percent."

She put down the remote and stared at the screen. Gabe looked good in his Armani suit. Better than good, on the steps of an impressive marble building with the wind barely ruffling his almost military style hair. Even more importantly, he looked confident, comfortable, jockeying questions from reporters with a host of supporters surrounding him. She caught glimpses of Gabe's boss, as well as Senator Humphries and a man she recognized as a former point guard for the New York Knicks.

You've done well, grasshopper. Her heart ached with a strange mixture of pride and regret. She'd been right. He was ready to fly solo.

"We've had eight successful years under Thaddeus Holcomb." Gabe motioned to his boss, who came to stand beside him. "I plan to build on that by working together with law enforcement and the community to make our streets the safest in the nation. That's why today I'm officially announcing my candidacy for New York County District Attorney. Thank you."

A few reporters tried to sneak in one last question, but they were drowned out by the applause of the crowd. Gabe strode down the stairs and off camera, shaking hands as he went, and the station cut back to the news anchors in studio.

"Turn that shit off." Freddie lurched on his stool, barely

catching himself before falling on his inebriated ass. "What happened to the game?"

"Game time's over for you, Freddie." She grabbed the remote and clicked until it landed on an old episode of *The Golden Girls*. That'd serve him right for complaining. Then she called the cab company.

"Drink up," she told him when she ended the call. "Taxi'll be here in ten."

After bringing the cops two more bottles of Yuengling, she headed around the bar to deal with a couple of newcomers at the table in the far corner. Dark suits, starched white shirts, power ties. Businessmen. Or lawyers. The Mark was popular with the legal set.

As she got closer, she could hear snippets of conversation.

"I don't know…nervous."

"…nothing to worry about."

"What if he…?"

"…told you…"

"…sure Nelson can't tie it to me?"

Devin froze. There must be hundreds of Nelsons in the Manhattan phone book. What were the odds they were talking about Gabe?

She ducked behind a pillar and listened, straining to catch every word.

"I've taken care of that. By the time I'm done with that security guard, no one will believe him, not even his own mother. Then they won't be able to tie the video tape to me. And if they can't tie it to me, they can't tie it to you."

The first voice was crisp, matter-of-fact and familiar. Devin shrank back farther behind the post.

"Sounds simple enough."

The second man spoke more deliberately, with a faint accent that sounded Eastern European.

"It is. My guys have dug up enough dirt on this guy

to bury him six times over. And if they need more, they know how to manufacture it."

"As long as you're sure…"

"Sure, I'm sure. No one will ever know we hid the surveillance tapes. And no one will figure out it's your son on the video. They'll never connect him to the murders."

"How can you be positive of that?"

"That's what the twenty grand was for. My contact at the lab will make it so no technology in existence could enhance that tape enough for anyone to identify Phillip."

"Thanks, Jack. I owe you one."

Jack. At least now she had a name.

"Let's see, you're endorsing me for DA and funding my political action committee…buy me a drink, and I think we can call it square."

DA?

"I would, if I could find the bartender. Doesn't anyone work around this place?"

Devin backed away slowly. When she was out of earshot, she hauled ass to the storeroom, where the manager was taking inventory.

"Al, I need you to wait on the guys at table three."

"I'm a little busy here." He held up a bottle of margarita mix, studied it for a second, then tossed it into the trash can next to him. "Expired. In 2010."

"I'll take over for you for a few minutes. Please. Just this one table." She raced over to the desk in the corner and started searching through the drawers for a pen and paper. No way was she disturbing Gabe at night, at home, and it'd be hours before she could see him at his office. She had to jot down what she'd heard while it was still fresh in her mind.

Shit, shit, shit. Why hadn't she thought to start the video rolling on her iPhone? Then she'd have hard evidence this Jack was fixing a case in order to win the election. Instead, Gabe would have to take her word for it. And she wasn't sure he'd trust her after she dumped him with virtually no explanation.

"Let me guess." Al smirked. "Ex boyfriend?"

"More like future ex cons."

Al threw another bottle into the garbage. "What's gotten into you? You've been acting weird all night."

"I'm fine." With one swoop of her arm, she cleared off the top of the desk and sat. Balancing the pad on one knee, she scrawled a few key words to help her remember what she'd heard.

Jack. DA. Surveillance tapes. Phillip. Murder.

When she was done, she looked up at Al, still sorting through the bottles on the storeroom shelves. "Are you going to help me or not?"

"Okay, I'll take care of your damn table." He took off his apron and straightened his shirt collar. "But after I'm done, you're going to tell me what's going on."

"Don't worry." She went back to her notes. "If things go as planned, you'll hear all about it on every news outlet in the tristate area."

"THERE'S SOMEONE HERE to see you."

Gabe looked up from the sentence he was reading for what must have been the tenth time to find his secretary standing in the doorway. "I thought I told you I didn't want to be disturbed," he snapped, his tone harsher than he'd intended.

Stephanie jerked her head back and her eyes widened.

Crap. He'd scared her. Again. He'd been a bear to work with since Devin dropped him like yesterday's *The Wall Street Journal*. Between his bad mood and the nonstop phone calls Stephanie had been forced to deal with in the wake of his announcement, it was a miracle she hadn't turned in her resignation.

Neither one of them had been able to get any work done, which meant Gabe hadn't figured out a way to connect Jack to the missing surveillance video. And until he did, an innocent man sat in jail.

"I'm sorry." Gabe gave his secretary what he hoped was a reassuring smile. "I know these past few weeks haven't been easy. And I trust your judgment. It must be important if you decided it was worth the interruption."

"She says it's urgent."

"She?"

"It's Devin. I tried to get her to leave a message or come back later, but she wouldn't take no for an answer."

A jolt of adrenaline kicked his heart into overdrive. He could picture her, hands on her hips, feet firmly planted, tapping one of her Doc Martens impatiently on the green-and-white linoleum.

It must be urgent for her to break down and pay him a visit. Like end-of-the-world urgent. He'd tried calling her so many times in the three weeks, two days, fourteen hours and fifty-three minutes since she'd walked out of his apartment—not that he was keeping track or anything—that it bordered on harassment. But she'd never answered. Hadn't returned any of his calls. Made it painfully clear she didn't want a damned thing to do with him. Only an act of God would have made her come all the way downtown to see him.

Had something happened to Victor? Or Leo? He didn't dare hope Devin had changed her mind and rushed to his side the minute she realized she'd made a huge mistake leaving him.

A sappy thought that suddenly didn't seem so sappy.

He saved the document he was working on and pushed his chair back. "That's Devin, all right. Show her in."

"I showed myself in." Devin pushed past Stephanie and made herself at home in one of his guest chairs, crossing one smooth, bare leg over the other and sending his sex drive into orbit. "I couldn't take the chance you wouldn't see me."

Gabe nodded to his secretary. "Thank you, Stephanie."

He cleared his throat and loosened his tie, fighting his more primal instincts, which were screaming at him to throw her across the desk and reenact the steamy sex dreams he'd been having on a nightly basis.

"I had to see you." Devin rummaged in her purse and pulled out a yellow legal pad. "It's urgent."

"So my secretary told me." Gabe picked up a pencil and twirled it in his fingers. "Must be to bring you down here."

"It's about the election."

He dropped the pencil. It bounced noisily on the desk, finally coming to rest next to his coffee cup. "The election?"

She nodded, her dark hair swinging. He was sure he could smell her almond shampoo, even across the desk. "Your opponent was at The Mark last night when I was tending bar."

"Jack?"

"That's him. He…"

Gabe held up his hand, palm out, silencing her.

"Hold on." He crossed to the door and checked the hall. Empty. With one final glance left and right to be sure no one was close by, he closed the door and returned to his seat.

"Now what's all this about?"

She pushed the pad across the desk. "I wrote it all down. I hope it's enough. I had my goddamn cell in my pocket the whole time, but I didn't think fast enough to hit Record."

He read silently, his mind whirring as he absorbed what she'd written.

"Did anyone else hear this?" he asked when he was finished.

She shook her head. "What does it all mean?"

"It's complicated. But with your help, I should be able to expose Jack and free an innocent man."

"And win the election," she added.

He shrugged. "That's secondary. Did you get a good look at either one of them?"

"No. And they didn't see me."

He damn well hoped not. Otherwise she could be in serious danger. There was no telling the lengths Jack would go to shut her up if he knew what she'd heard. "Do you think you could identify their voices?"

"Probably." She frowned, her forehead creasing in concentration. "The first one sounded familiar, and the minute the second guy called him Jack it clicked. I met him that day in your office. And the other guy had an accent. Eastern European, I think. But I'd know his voice if I heard it again."

Eastern European accent, with a son named Phillip? And enough money and influence to have an assistant district attorney in his pocket? That could only be one guy. Ilya Roginsky, real estate mogul and owner of half the island of Manhattan.

Shit. Gabe steepled his fingers under his chin. Roginsky was rumored to have connections with the Russian mob. Jack was small potatoes compared to him.

"Are you willing to swear to that under oath?" he asked. "Give a statement to my inspector? Testify in court if it comes to that?"

He hoped to hell it wouldn't. And if it did, he'd make damned sure she had a security detail around the clock. If anything happened to her... He ran a hand through his hair, not even able to contemplate what he'd do then.

Her bottom lip trembled for a split second before she

pressed her mouth into a tight, thin line. "If that's what it takes. So you believe me?"

"Of course. Why wouldn't I?"

"I don't know, maybe because I broke up with you, didn't return any of your phone calls and showed up here unannounced, with some chicken scratch on a legal pad?"

He let out his breath in a long whoosh. "Whatever happened between us, you're no liar. I'd stake my career on that."

"Thanks." She twisted one of the studs in her ear and looked away. "I want you to know…"

A rap at the door cut her off.

"Come in," Gabe called.

Jack stuck his oily head in. "What's with all the closed doors lately?"

His eyes landed on Devin. "Never mind. Now I understand. Sorry for interrupting."

"I'm sure you are." Gabe wrapped his fingers around the arms of his chair in a white-knuckle grip, resisting the urge to jump over the desk and pound Jack's smug face into a pulp. The instant gratification would be sweet, but seeing Jack escorted out of the office in handcuffs would be the best revenge. "At least you had the courtesy to knock this time."

"Stephanie said you have the transcripts of the Reyes trial." Jack crossed to the empty guest chair and made himself at home, sinking into it and resting an ankle on one knee.

Gabe gritted his teeth. "Stephanie also knows I don't want to be disturbed."

"I dimly recall her mentioning something about that." Jack waved off Gabe's complaint. "But I need to read the testimony of the defense's expert tonight. I'm cross-examining him in the Samuels case tomorrow."

"I'll have her bring it to you when we're done."

Devin unfolded her long legs and rose. "It's okay. I think I've got what I need."

Her eyes caught Gabe's and she nodded, telling him without words she'd heard enough. Jack was one of the men at The Mark last night. He nodded back, letting her know he understood.

"What you need?" Jack waggled his eyebrows.

"Get your mind out of the gutter." Devin shot him a glare that could have turned the Hope Diamond into a pile of expensive dust. "Gabe was giving me some friendly legal advice. Landlord issues."

She turned to Gabe, her expression softening. "Thanks again."

"My pleasure." Gabe stood and walked her to the door. When they got there, he bent his head to whisper in her ear. "I'll be in touch so we can take your statement. About your landlord."

"Gabe." Her voice faltered and she started again. "Gabe, I'm…"

"Sorry. I know." He reached for the door knob and pulled the door open.

She gave him a weak smile and strode through.

And for the second time in a month he stood and watched helplessly as the woman he loved walked away.

19

"WHAT ARE YOU making for us today, Victor?"

Devin looked over Victor's shoulder at the drawing on the table in front of him. This had become a Thursday ritual in the months since she'd found her brother. She picked him up at Haven House in the morning and brought him to Ink the Heights. He seemed to like the atmosphere of the shop—the yellow walls cheery but not too bright, the customers chatty but not too friendly.

Then, when her shift was done, she took him back to the group home. It made for a long day traveling to and from Long Island, and she had to borrow Leo's car, which she hated. But that would change once a space in their Manhattan location opened up, something the staff at Haven House assured her would happen any day now, maybe even in time for Christmas. From there, the plan was for him to move in with Devin, eventually, with the help of a full-time aide.

"Seahorse," Victor answered, not looking up from his artwork, his colored pencil moving furiously. Eye contact was still tough for him. But he remembered her. Responded to her questions. Even let her touch him every once in a while.

"It's beautiful," she said. He'd rendered the creature in muted blues and greens, flanked by pale yellow sea grass and bright pink and purple coral.

"Another one for the book?" Leo asked, coming over to see for himself. Ever since Victor's second visit, when Leo had seen him doodling on a napkin with a Sharpie and given him paper and a set of colored pencils, Leo had taken a special interest in Victor's artistic ability. Just like he'd done with Devin ten years ago.

"I'd say so." Devin laid her hand gently on her brother's shoulder. Her heart stuttered when he didn't flinch.

"I'll get it." Leo went and pulled down a thick black binder, already bursting at the seams. "We're going to need another one soon. The regulars will revolt if we don't have Victor's latest designs to show them."

"What do you think, Victor?" Devin asked. "Should we start a new book? Maybe a red binder this time. You can do some special stuff for the holidays."

Christmas had always been his favorite time of year. Santa Claus. Snowflakes. Sleigh bells. He loved it all, in small doses. "And we can decorate the shop next week."

Victor's eyes stayed locked on the drawing but his head gave an almost imperceptible nod. "The male seahorse is the only male in the animal kingdom to give birth to its young."

"Where did you learn that?" She let her hand fall, not wanting to push her luck.

"Animal Planet." He finished shading a blade of sea grass and put down his pencil. "I also know that seahorses are fish, that they're bad swimmers and that they mate for life."

"Let me guess." She smiled. "More Animal Planet?"

"Is Leo your mate?" He picked up an orange pencil and started on another piece of coral.

"I'm her friend." Leo thankfully stepped in to respond, setting the binder down gently on the table so as not to startle Victor. "Yours, too."

"You should have a mate. For life, like seahorses." Victor caught her eye briefly then looked back down at his paper. "What about Gabe? He could be your mate."

Her brother had only met Gabe a few times in the weeks before the split, but Gabe had clearly made quite an impression, judging by the number of times Victor brought his name up. Each new reference was like a knife to the gut, hot and twisting. She thought the pain would recede with time. If anything, it had gotten worse. Two months of intense, bittersweet longing, from the roots of her hair to the tips of her Pamplona Purple toenails.

"He has a point." Leo rested against the wall, crossing his tattooed arms across his broad chest and giving her what she called his Spanish Inquisition stare. "You never did tell me what went wrong with you and Clarence Darrow."

"It's complicated."

"It always is."

"It was for the best."

"Who's best?" Leo's eyes narrowed. "Yours? Because I hate to tell you, *hermanita*, I've seen you in far better shape. You've been sleepwalking through life since you two broke up."

"I have not."

"Then why did you almost misspell *strength* on Jazmin's wrist?"

"Spelling's never been my strong suit." Devin grabbed a handful of tools from her work station, tossed them into the autoclave and flipped the switch. "And I caught it in time, didn't I?"

"Barely."

"I'm done." Victor slid his drawing across the table. "And I'm hungry."

"I've got granola bars in my purse." Devin reached under the table for her bag. "That'll have to tide you over until closing time."

"Go." Leo picked up the drawing and admired it, sliding the paper into an empty sheet protector. "I'll lock up. Looks like my last client's a no-show."

As he spoke, the bell above the door chimed. A second later, Hector pushed through the curtain and dropped into Leo's hydraulic chair. "Sorry I'm late, *manito*."

"Gabe," Victor said.

"Not Gabe." Hector had about ten years and fifty pounds on Gabe. Maybe Victor wasn't as enamored with Gabe as she thought if he'd mixed them up. Then again, the workings of Victor's mind were—and would always be—a mystery. "This is Hector. You've seen him here before. He's getting your wolf tattooed on his shoulder."

"No. Gabe." Victor pointed to a newspaper someone had left behind. "Here."

"In the paper?" Devin crouched next to her brother for a better view. "Let me see."

Gabe had been big news since the shitstorm with Jack hit the fan. He'd come out the hero, with Jack disgraced, forced to resign and possibly facing criminal charges. And even more important in Gabe's eyes, she knew, the suspect in the Park Avenue case had been released and reunited with his family. Maybe they'd finally tracked down Phillip and arrested him.

She inched the newspaper out from under Victor's hand. Sure enough, Gabe's face stared back at her, handsome as always but haggard, recent events clearly taking their toll. But the headline next to the photo wasn't about Phillip or the Park Avenue murders. Instead, it read Front Runner May Be Bowing out of Race for Top Spot in DA's Office.

She shot upright, banging her hip on the table and almost knocking Victor's pencils onto the floor. "What the fuck?"

"That's a bad word." Her brother rocked back and forth. "You're not supposed to say bad words."

"I know. But sometimes…" Sometimes even *fuck* wasn't strong enough to express her level of pissedoffed-ness. Sometimes a thousand fucks weren't strong enough.

"Que pasa?" Leo put the binder back on the shelf and leaned against the counter.

"Take a look at this." She thrust the paper into his hands. "He's quitting."

"Who's quitting what?" Hector asked.

Devin ignored him and sat on the edge of her tattoo chair to stop herself from pacing the floor, which would only make Victor nervous. "All that work getting him ready to run, for nothing. How can he do this to me?"

"To you?" Leo raised a suspicious brow. "Or for you?"

"What's that supposed to mean?"

"Did you read the article?"

"No." She'd been too freaking furious to get past the headline.

"It says he's considering dropping out to focus on personal issues," Leo read. "Rumor has it he's heartbroken."

"It does not say that." She snatched the paper back, frantically scanning it.

"Not in so many words," Leo admitted. "But the picture speaks volumes. Look at those haunted eyes. If that's not a man who's had his heart ripped out and stomped on, I don't know what is."

"I did not rip out his heart and stomp on it." Devin huffed a stray hair off her forehead. "And heartbroken or not, I'm not letting him quit. Not after I left him so he'd…"

Damn. She bit her lip, but it was too late. The knowing glint in Leo's eyes told her she'd already said too much.

"Ah." His satisfied smile would have rivaled the Cheshire cat's. "Now we're getting somewhere."

Hector coughed not so discretely. "Can someone please tell me what's going on?"

"Devin gave up the man she loves under the misguided impression that she's bad for his career. And now he's giving up his career for her." Leo put the newspaper down on the counter behind him and walked over to his station. "Very 'The Gift of the Magi.'"

"That's not it at all."

"Isn't it?" Leo tilted his head to study her. "It's obvious to even the most casual observer."

"Obvious," Victor echoed, methodically putting his pencils back in their box.

She shook her head. It couldn't be. Yeah, she loved him. That much of Leo's theory was true. But no way was he dropping out of the race for her. There had to be some other reason. And as much as she hated the idea of facing him again, there was only one way to find out.

Ask him.

"I'm still not following you," Hector said, rubbing his jaw.

"And I'm still hungry." Victor snapped the lid on his pencil box shut.

"Here." Devin fished another granola bar out of her purse. "Your favorite. Chocolate chip and peanut butter."

Victor knocked it out of her hand. "I don't want granola. I want McDonald's."

She looked at the clock above the sink. 6:05 p.m. Too late to catch Gabe at the office, and no way was she going to his apartment. Too many memories and way, way too much room for temptation, with his ginormous bed and the walk-in shower with the body jets. Besides, she had to get Victor fed and home. Anything she had to say to Gabe would have to wait until tomorrow, when she'd had time to calm down and think rationally.

"Come on." She picked up the granola bar, stuffed it

into her purse and handed her brother his backpack and Tex. The armadillo hadn't been out of his sight since she'd given it back to him. "Let's get our coats and grab something to eat."

"Hermanita." Leo's voice was soft but insistent, stopping her in her tracks. "If you love him, go to him. Fix this before it's too late."

A shadow crossed his face, and not for the first time she wondered what romantic skeletons were hiding in Leo's closet.

"What if you're right?" she asked, the words almost catching in her throat. "What if he really is giving it all up for me?"

"Then he's your seahorse. Your mate," Victor said. In a rare moment of real connection, her brother's eyes met hers, and the raw honesty, the trust, the understanding she saw there floored her. "For life."

"I'M SORRY, BUT YOU just missed him."

"Shit." Devin scuffed the toe of her boot on the linoleum. "Are you sure you can't catch him? I only need a minute. It's…"

"Let me guess. It's urgent." Gabe's secretary gave her a patronizing smile. "Again."

"Yeah, like last time." Devin knew she sounded like a goddamned broken record, but she was way past caring. All that mattered was getting to Gabe ASAP so she could stop him from throwing away everything he'd worked so hard for. "It's about the election."

"Then it won't be urgent for much longer. Gabe's about to give a press conference. He's withdrawing from the race."

Fuck. This was even worse than she thought. He wasn't just considering dropping out. He was actually doing it. Today.

"He can't quit," Devin insisted. "I have to stop him."

The secretary pressed her lips into a thin, harsh line. "Good luck with that. He's on his way to city hall. He'll be half way through his speech by the time you get there."

"City hall?"

"He's giving a statement to the press and filing the withdrawal papers with the clerk's office."

"What time?"

"You'll never make it."

"What time?" Devin repeated even louder.

"His speech starts in ten minutes."

"Thanks," Devin grumbled. "For nothing."

"Wait."

Devin turned, hands on her hips. "This better be worth every second it's costing me."

"Here." The secretary came out from behind her desk and handed Devin a plastic identification card on a mint green lanyard. "Take this."

"What is it?"

"Press pass. It'll get you past security."

Devin lowered her head to stare at the other woman. "What gives? Now you want to help me?"

"Let's just say I have a feeling work will be a lot more pleasant if you're back with Gabe."

"Who said anything about me getting back with Gabe?"

"Why else would you race downtown to stop him from committing political suicide? And he's been unbearable since you guys split." She nudged Devin toward the elevators. "Now go. Fast. Stop him before he files those papers."

"Thanks," Devin said, meaning it this time.

She didn't stop running when she hit the street, racing all of the six plus blocks to City Hall, thankful every step of the way she'd traded her thigh-high stiletto boots for a pair of Docs just before leaving her apartment. It was like some inner voice was telling her she'd need speed more than sex appeal to fix this mess.

She'd also need the right words, which she didn't have yet, and the guts to say them in front of a pack of strangers. And a lot of luck to get there and track down Gabe before it was too late.

Any worry that she'd have trouble finding him in the maze of corridors and offices that made up city hall vanished the second she turned the corner and saw the crowd on the massive steps leading up to the building's main entrance. The same steps where Gabe had announced his candidacy on television almost two months ago. News vans from all of the major stations sat parked at the curb, their antennas whirling.

And on top of the stairs, at the center of it all, stood Gabe behind a wooden podium, a gray wool coat over his usual suit, one hand thrust in his pocket, looking like a modern-day Atticus Finch. Several other well-dressed gentlemen surrounded him. One she recognized as his boss, but unlike last time the rest of the men were unfamiliar. Devin rubbed her hands together, trying not to attach too much significance to the fact that the heavy hitters were noticeably absent.

"We're here for two reasons today," Gabe began. "First, we've made an arrest in the Park Avenue homicide case."

Her heart pounded even faster than it already was from her six-block sprint. He hadn't announced that he was dropping out yet. She wasn't too late.

She breathed in the cool, fall air and let it out in a long, slow hiss. She'd faced plenty of scary-ass situations in her twenty-eight years. Taking care of her stoned mother. Having Victor ripped out of her arms and taken away from her. Sleeping on the street, alone and cold.

This topped them all.

She pushed her way through the crowd as Gabe continued to discuss the arrest, desperate to get to the front before he started in on the election.

"I'm sorry, miss." A thick-necked man with Security written across the chest of his navy blue windbreaker stopped her with an outstretched arm. "Press only past this point."

She flashed the pass around her neck with a cocky grin she hoped said "ace reporter."

The security guard frowned. "Which outlet?"

Shit. She hadn't thought of that.

"Uh, *The Village Voice.*" Hopefully he'd believe the alternative weekly tabloid would employ someone with four earrings in one ear and a spider-web tattoo.

"Go ahead." He lowered his arm and she made her way up the steps.

She stopped about halfway up and listened, staying partially hidden in the crowd. She kept quiet as Gabe fielded questions about the murders. After a few minutes of answering what seemed like the same question asked ten different ways, he ran a hand through his hair and scanned the crowd.

"If there's nothing more on the Park Avenue case, I'll move on to the second reason I brought you here today." He paused to take a sip of water from a bottle on the podium. "It's with a heavy heart and after much consideration that I've decided to—"

"Stop." Devin shoved past the people standing in front of her so she stood alone, exposed. He'd made the choice for her. It was now or never. And never wasn't an option. "Don't do it."

Gabe's eyes found hers. She could hear the footsteps of the security goons and their muffled "make ways" and "coming throughs" as they tried to reach her, but she didn't flinch. Her feet stayed firmly planted, her gaze locked on Gabe.

"Don't quit." Her words tumbled out, racing to be heard before the guards got to her and shut her down. "The city needs you."

Gabe's eyes darkened and he stepped away from the podium. "There's only one person in this city I want to need me."

"I need you. I…"

Her words ended in a groan as one of the guards yanked her hands behind her back. "Press my ass. You're busted, sweetheart."

"What, no handcuffs?" she quipped.

"I'm only authorized to escort you peacefully from the premises. Unless you'd like me to get the police involved."

"Let her go." Gabe raced down the steps to Devin, his clipped tone saying that he meant business. "She's with me."

The guard hesitated a moment then released her and moved away, staying close enough to restrain her if things went south. A second guard appeared and stood next to him.

Two on one. How was that fair?

"And I, for one, want to hear what she has to say," Gabe continued, his voice lower, more tender, his focus back on Devin and not the brute squad.

"You're really going to make me do this here? In front of everyone?"

Gabe smiled and crossed his arms. Smug bastard.

"Okay, fine. If that's how you want it." She took a deep, shuddering breath and plunged forward. "I love you, dammit. That's why I can't stand by and watch you give up."

The smile playing about his lips turned from smug to sincere. "Only you can say 'I love you' and curse in the same sentence and make it sound romantic."

"You see? That's exactly why I left." She waved her arms in a gesture that screamed crazy bag lady. "I swear

too much. I dress all wrong. I'm about as far from a political asset as you can get. I didn't want to cost you your
dream. And now you're throwing it away anyway."

"Don't you get it? You are my dream. The rest of it's
crap without you."

She shook her head. "You don't mean that."

"I can and I do." He took her cheeks in his palms, meeting her gaze. "If I have to choose, my choice will be the
same every damn time. I choose you. I love you."

She closed her eyes. It was nice to hear the words, but
she didn't need them. It was her she'd doubted, not him.
But she was through doubting. Through questioning. She
was running on raw emotion now. "What if you didn't
have to choose?"

"Hey," one of the reporters on the other side of the
crowd shouted before Gabe could answer. "We can't hear
you."

"Yeah, what's going on?"

"Who's the girl?"

"Are you dropping out of the race or not?"

"You tell me." Gabe lowered his forehead to hers. "Am
I quitting or not?"

"No." Devin pulled back so she could look at him.
Her heart squeezed in her chest at what she saw on his
handsome face: vulnerability, resolve, but mostly pure,
unconditional love.

She grabbed Gabe's hand and dragged him back up the
stairs to the podium. "Definitely not," she said into the
microphone for the benefit of the fourth estate.

"You don't have to do this." He covered the mike with
his hand. "I don't have to run."

"Yes, you do. Serving the public is what you do. It's
who you are. I don't want to change that. Just don't blame
me and my big mouth if you lose." She gave him a saucy
smile and a shrug.

"I like your big mouth," he murmured, wrapping his arms around her and holding her so tightly it almost hurt. "And how can I lose when I've already won?"

"Kiss her," someone yelled.

"Yeah, kiss her." Another man joined in and within seconds the entire crowd was chanting, "Kiss her, kiss her."

"What do you think?" he asked. "Should we give them what they want?"

"Well…" She looked down at the crowd then back up at Gabe, loving the way his eyes devoured her with not only desire but affection. "They are the public. And you are their servant."

"No." His lips hovered inches from hers. "I'm yours."

"I like the sound of that." Tears pricked her eyes and for the first time in her life she didn't try to blink them away. Let Gabe see—let everyone see—how much he affected her. "Now shut up and kiss me so we can get the hell out of here—" Devin dropped her voice to a whisper "—and I can have my wicked way with you."

Hell, it had been almost two months since they'd gotten naked together. And that was almost two months too long, if you asked her.

He smiled against her lips a second before claiming them in a kiss filled with tenderness and heat and promises for the future. "Now that I like the sound of."

Epilogue

"KEEP YOUR EYES CLOSED, dammit!" Devin laughed as she guided Gabe up the steps. "It's supposed to be a surprise."

"What is?"

"If I told you, it wouldn't be a surprise. Besides, we're almost there." She pulled out the key Graham had given her and unlocked the door.

"Just make sure I don't run into anything."

Devin scanned the large, empty room. "I don't think that will be a problem."

She stepped inside, bringing him with her. "You can open them now."

Gabe swiveled his head, no doubt taking in the bare, white walls, the gleaming wood floor and the lack of anything else. "It's… charming. But we have an apartment. With furniture."

Her insides warmed at the thought of the cozy two-bedroom they'd picked out together on the upper west side, halfway between his office and Ink the Heights. She'd stopped tending bar for now, focusing on tattooing and…other pursuits. Like the one that had brought them to an empty room in Soho. "It's not ours. And it's not to live in."

"Then what's it for?"

"It's a gallery. Called Esoterica. Or will be, once Graham gets it up and running in a few months. And guess who's going to be the featured artist on opening night?"

"You?"

Devin nodded. "My first show."

With a whoop, Gabe picked her up and twirled her around. When he set her down, still in the circle of his arms, he planted a wet, smacking kiss on her lips. "I'm so proud of you, babe. I knew you could do it."

"That makes one of us." She reached up to caress his cheek. "Thanks for pushing me. I couldn't have done it without you."

"Yes, you could have. But I'm glad you didn't have to." He kissed her again. "What do you say we go tell Victor?"

She smiled, loving that his first thought was of her brother. But telling Victor could wait until morning. He was with his friends at his new group home. And she had plans for Gabe.

"I've got a better idea. How about we celebrate with dinner at Sura Thai. And dessert in bed."

"Smart girl." He slid his hands down her back to cup her bottom. "Must be why I fell in love with you."

"You mean it wasn't for my rocking bod?" She moved against him, and she could feel the evidence of his arousal pressing hot and hard on her thigh. "Or my ability to sway voters your way, Mr. District Attorney?"

"Those are just fringe benefits. And I'm not DA yet."

"You will be. You're miles ahead in the polls."

"Let's hope I stay there." He released her and grabbed her hand, pulling her to the door. "Come on, let's go. The sooner we eat dinner, the sooner we'll get to dessert."

"Or we could skip dinner altogether." She gave him her most seductive, come-hither look.

He grinned. "Even better."

"I just have to lock up and leave the key for Graham."

"Graham? Isn't that…"

"Ivy's friend. He's striking out on his own."

"You contacted him? I thought you didn't want to ride on anyone's coattails."

"I was being stupid and shortsighted. Like you said, we all need help from our friends sometimes." She bolted the door and dropped the key through the slot in the locked mailbox.

"You've got a veritable army in your corner now, sweetheart." Gabe took her hand and twined their fingers together. Her heart skipped a beat, like it always did when he touched her. "The Nelsons are a force to be reckoned with."

"There's only one Nelson I need on my side." She leaned her head on his shoulder. "And he's right here."

"To stay." He kissed her forehead and started down the steps, leading Devin along with him. "Now, about that dessert…"

* * * * *

REQUEST YOUR FREE BOOKS!
2 FREE NOVELS PLUS 2 FREE GIFTS!

HARLEQUIN®

Blaze

red-hot reads!

YES! Please send me 2 FREE Harlequin® Blaze® novels and my 2 FREE gifts (gifts are worth about $10). After receiving them, if I don't wish to receive any more books, I can return the shipping statement marked "cancel." If I don't cancel, I will receive 4 brand-new novels every month and be billed just $4.74 per book in the U.S. or $5.21 per book in Canada. That's a savings of at least 14% off the cover price. It's quite a bargain. Shipping and handling is just 50¢ per book in the U.S. and 75¢ per book in Canada.* I understand that accepting the 2 free books and gifts places me under no obligation to buy anything. I can always return a shipment and cancel at any time. Even if I never buy another book, the two free books and gifts are mine to keep forever.

150/350 HDN GH2D

Name	(PLEASE PRINT)	
Address		Apt. #
City	State/Prov.	Zip/Postal Code

Signature (if under 18, a parent or guardian must sign)

Mail to the **Reader Service:**
IN U.S.A.: P.O. Box 1867, Buffalo, NY 14240-1867
IN CANADA: P.O. Box 609, Fort Erie, Ontario L2A 5X3

Want to try two free books from another line?
Call 1-800-873-8635 or visit www.ReaderService.com.

* Terms and prices subject to change without notice. Prices do not include applicable taxes. Sales tax applicable in N.Y. Canadian residents will be charged applicable taxes. Offer not valid in Quebec. This offer is limited to one order per household. Not valid for current subscribers to Harlequin Blaze books. All orders subject to credit approval. Credit or debit balances in a customer's account(s) may be offset by any other outstanding balance owed by or to the customer. Please allow 4 to 6 weeks for delivery. Offer available while quantities last.

Your Privacy—The Reader Service is committed to protecting your privacy. Our Privacy Policy is available online at www.ReaderService.com or upon request from the Reader Service.

We make a portion of our mailing list available to reputable third parties that offer products we believe may interest you. If you prefer that we not exchange your name with third parties, or if you wish to clarify or modify your communication preferences, please visit us at www.ReaderService.com/consumerschoice or write to us at Reader Service Preference Service, P.O. Box 9062, Buffalo, NY 14240-9062. Include your complete name and address.

HB15

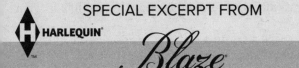
"Keep looking at me that way and we're going to do something we'll both regret."

Avery jerked her gaze from Knox's bare chest to his eyes. "How am I looking at you?"

"Like you want to run that gorgeous mouth all over me."

"Hmm…maybe I do." She could hear her own words, a little slow, a little slurred.

"You're drunk, Doc."

Flopping back onto the sand, Avery propped her head against Knox's thigh.

She stared up at him, his head haloed by the black sky and twinkling stars. They both seemed so far away— Knox and the heavens.

"I've never gotten drunk and made bad decisions before," she said. "Was hoping we could make one together."

He made a sound, a cross between a laugh, a wheeze and a groan. "What kind of bad decision did you have in mind?"

"Oh, you know, giving in to the sexual tension that's been clawing at us since the day we met. But I guess you're not drunk enough yet to want me."

"Trust me when I say I don't have to be drunk to want you, Avery."

She made a scoffing sound. "You don't even like me."

Slowly, Knox smoothed his hand across her face, fingers gliding from cheekbone to forehead to chin.

"I like you just fine, Doc," he whispered, his voice gruff and smoky. The words spilled across her skin like warm honey.

He growled low in his throat. His palm landed on her belly, spreading wide and applying the slightest pressure. "I'm fighting to do the right thing."

"What if I don't want you to do the right thing?"

She felt the tremor in his hand, the commanding force weighing her down. If he stopped touching her she might float off into the night and never find her way back.

"I don't take advantage of women who are inebriated." His words were harsh, but his eyes glowed as they stared down at her. Devoured her.

Never in her life had she felt so…desired. And she wanted that. Wanted him.

"Please."

Avery was certain that in the morning she'd hate herself for that single word and how close she sounded to begging. But right now, she didn't care.

"Please," she whispered again, just to make sure he knew she meant it.

Don't miss
IN TOO DEEP by Kira Sinclair,
available July 2015 wherever
Harlequin® Blaze® books and ebooks are sold.